This is a work of fiction. Similarities to real people, places, or events are entirely coincidental.

THE WITCH NEXT DOOR

First edition. February 10, 2024.

Copyright © 2024 Nathaniel Baker.

ISBN: 979-8224162000

Written by Nathaniel Baker.

THE WITCH NEXT DOOR

Chapter 1: The Substitute

Jefferson High School buzzed with the energy of students rushing through crowded hallways. Lockers slammed shut, laughter echoed, and friendships formed visible bonds. Yet, for Gal, the atmosphere was one of isolation and resentment. The once unbreakable trio of friends—Gal, Jane, and Sue—had shattered, leaving her to navigate the turbulent sea of high school alone.

Gal's footsteps echoed a melancholic rhythm as she trudged through the labyrinthine corridors. Her thoughts were consumed by the growing distance between her and her former best friends. Jane and Sue, once inseparable companions, had become strangers, their camaraderie replaced by an unspoken tension.

As Gal entered the English classroom, the familiar scent of books and chalk filled the air. However, the sense of comfort she once found in this room had dissipated. A new figure stood at the front, a substitute teacher named Ms. Hassan. Something about Ms. Hassan's piercing gaze unsettled Gal, who quickly took her seat.

The substitute wasted no time in making herself known. Inquiring about Mr. Willoughby, the English teacher now in a coma, Ms. Hassan displayed an unusual interest in Gal's connection with him. Gal, grappling with her own emotions and the complexities of teenage friendships, couldn't help but feel a strange pull towards this enigmatic teacher.

After class, as the bell rang and the corridors flooded with students, Ms. Hassan approached Gal. The substitute's words hung in the air like a mysterious invitation, promising a solution to the predicament surrounding Mr. Willoughby.

Curiosity mingled with desperation, Gal found herself accepting the invitation to Ms. Hassan's home. Little did she know, this decision would plunge her into a surreal journey that transcended the boundaries of the known world.

That evening, Gal, driven by a mix of hope and apprehension, sneaked out of her house to meet Ms. Hassan. The night sky hung heavy with secrets, mirroring the uncertainty that awaited her. As she approached Ms. Hassan's residence, a sense of foreboding settled over her, but the allure of a possible solution for Mr. Willoughby urged her forward.

Entering Ms. Hassan's home, Gal was greeted by an ambiance that seemed to hum with mystical energy. The air was thick with unfamiliar scents, and the flickering candlelight cast dancing shadows on the walls. Gal couldn't shake the feeling that she had stepped into a realm where the ordinary rules of existence no longer applied.

Ms. Hassan, draped in an aura of mystery, revealed herself to be more than just a substitute teacher. With a voice that resonated with power, she unveiled a task of otherworldly proportions. The three friends were to retrieve three amulets scattered across different dimensions, promising that these artifacts held the key to granting their deepest desires.

In a blink, the room transformed, and Gal found herself standing on the precipice of a journey that would challenge not only the fabric of reality but also the bonds of friendship that had been strained to their limits.

Little did she know, the odyssey set in motion by the mysterious substitute teacher would lead her through haunted mansions, zombie-infested islands, and eerie cornfields. The quest for the amulets would unravel secrets, test the resilience of friendship, and force her to confront not only external adversaries but also the demons within.

As Gal took the first step into this fantastical adventure, she couldn't fathom the extent to which her life was about to change. The substitute had become the harbinger of a tale that transcended the mundane, weaving a narrative where magic and reality danced in precarious harmony, and the pursuit of one's desires came at a cost unimaginable.

Chapter 1 marked the inception of a journey into the unknown, a journey where the boundaries between the tangible and the fantastical blurred, and Gal's fate became intertwined with the mystical forces that lurked in the shadows. Little did she know that the substitute had set in motion a sequence of events that would redefine not only her understanding of the world but also the very essence of her existence.

As Gal delved deeper into this surreal expedition, she couldn't shake the feeling that each step she took led her further away from the familiar contours of reality. The air crackled with an energy unknown to her, as if the very fabric of existence quivered in response to the cosmic forces at play.

Ms. Hassan, the orchestrator of this mystical quest, guided Gal through the intricacies of the first dimension. The graveyard she and her friends landed in held echoes of a tragic past. Haunted mansions and ethereal entities surrounded them, revealing fragments of a story that transcended the boundaries of life and death.

In the search for the first amulet, Gal and her companions encountered spectral apparitions bound to the mansion. Whispers of a dark family legacy lingered in the air, unveiling the sinister history that intertwined with the amulets they sought. With each revelation, the trio's understanding of their quest deepened, and the stakes grew higher.

The journey through the haunted mansion was not merely a physical exploration but a descent into the recesses of their own fears and insecurities. Gal, haunted by the fractured friendship with Jane and Sue, confronted the ghosts of her past, both literal and metaphorical.

As the trio touched the first amulet, the barriers between the dimensions quivered, and they found themselves propelled into another reality.

The shift was instantaneous. From the spectral ambiance of the mansion, they emerged on a deserted beach, the rhythmic waves serving as a backdrop to a macabre scene. A luxury cruise liner, laden with zombies, ran aground on the island. The second dimension presented a stark contrast to the eerie tranquility of the graveyard, plunging Gal and her friends into a battle against the undead.

Jane, Sue, and Gal, armed with newfound strength and resilience, fought off the zombie horde. The undead were relentless, their relentless pursuit driven by the enigmatic Zombie Queen—the horrifying manifestation of Ms. Hassan herself. The second amulet, worn by the Zombie Queen, became the focal point of their struggle.

In a desperate gambit, Sue volunteered to stay behind, diverting the attention of the zombie horde. Jane and Gal, navigating the dilapidated remains of the cruise liner, confronted the Zombie Queen. A harrowing battle ensued, and just as victory seemed within reach, a new threat emerged.

From the remains of the Zombie Queen, a Zombie Baby—bearer of the stolen amulet—scuttled away. The pursuit of the amulet led Jane and Gal through the labyrinthine bowels of the ship, where every shadow seemed to conceal a new danger. The echoes of their footsteps were drowned by the moans of the undead, creating a symphony of dread that reverberated through the vessel.

The climax of their struggle played out on the blood-stained decks of the cruise liner, culminating in the transformation of Sue into one of the undead. The emotional weight of witnessing a friend succumb to the zombie curse added a layer of tragedy to their already perilous journey.

As Gal and Jane landed in the third dimension, an eerie cornfield and farm awaited them, haunted by spectral children with a haunting past. Amidst the stalks that whispered of ancient curses, they encountered Sackface—a chainsaw-wielding killer whose motives aligned with their own. United against a common enemy, Gal and Jane forged an uneasy alliance with Jacob, a missing person from their home dimension.

In the barn where the confrontation with Zombie Sue reached its climax, the trio discovered a crucial revelation. The children of the corn, the spectral inhabitants of this dimension, held the key to unlocking the whereabouts of the third amulet. The realization dawned that their quest was not merely a journey to collect artifacts; it was a battle against the witch's curse that had ensnared generations in a cyclical nightmare.

Gal's determination, fueled by the resilience of newfound allies and the ghosts of her own past, brought them closer to their goal. The cryptic clues provided by the children of the corn guided them through the haunting landscape, pushing the boundaries of their understanding of magic and malevolence.

With the third amulet within reach, Gal, Jane, and Jacob prepared to return to their home dimension. The threads of destiny, interwoven with the mystical forces at play, hinted at a resolution that could alter the course of their lives forever.

As they faced the vortex that would transport them back to the familiar world, Gal couldn't shake the feeling that the layers of reality were thinning, revealing glimpses of a cosmic tapestry where their destinies were but threads in an intricate design.

Little did they know that their return would usher in a confrontation with Ms. Hassan, the malevolent force orchestrating this mystical chessboard. The stage was set for a final reckoning—one that would test the limits of friendship, unravel the mysteries of the amulets, and unveil the true nature of the witch next door.

As Gal, Jane, and Jacob emerged from the vortex, the familiar surroundings of Ms. Hassan's home greeted them. The air crackled with an ominous tension, as if the very walls harbored the echoes of countless secrets. Yet, there was no sign of Ms. Hassan or any imminent threat.

Gal's gaze darted around the room, her senses heightened by the impending confrontation. The flicker of candlelight danced on the walls, casting eerie shadows that seemed to writhe with a life of their own. It was a silence pregnant with anticipation, the calm before the storm.

Then, with a spectral grace, Ms. Hassan materialized before them. Her presence exuded a malevolence that seemed to seep into every corner of the room. Her eyes, devoid of humanity, fixated on the trio with a predatory gleam.

MS. HASSAN

Welcome back, my little pawns. I trust your journey has been enlightening?

Her voice, a melodic symphony laced with a sinister undertone, echoed through the room. Gal, Jane, and Jacob stood firm, the weight of their shared experiences forging an unspoken bond that defied the supernatural forces at play.

JACOB

(eyeing Ms. Hassan)

Your twisted game ends here. We've retrieved your precious trinkets, but we won't be handing them over.

Gal, fueled by a newfound determination, stepped forward. The three amulets, glinting with an otherworldly glow, were clutched in her hands. The source of Ms. Hassan's power lay within those artifacts, and now, they held the key to her undoing.

GAL

We've seen the darkness you've hidden, the suffering you've caused. It ends now.

Ms. Hassan's lips curled into a malevolent smile, her demeanor shifting from composed elegance to a primal anticipation. The room seemed to contract, the walls closing in as if mirroring the escalating tension.

MS. HASSAN

Ah, the audacity of mortals. Do you truly believe you can defy fate? These amulets were always meant to be mine.

With a swift motion, Gal, Jane, and Jacob positioned themselves in a triangle, each holding one of the amulets. The room quivered as the amulets resonated with a harmonious frequency, a counterpoint to Ms. Hassan's malevolent aura.

GAL

(voice resolute)

If we can't stop you, then at least we'll go down fighting.

In unison, they chanted an incantation, a blend of ancient words and shared determination. The amulets pulsed with an ethereal light, forging a protective barrier that repelled Ms. Hassan's malevolent influence.

The room became a battleground of opposing forces, a clash between the relentless pursuit of power and the resilience of those who sought to defy it. Ms. Hassan, undeterred, summoned arcane energies, attempting to breach the protective barrier.

Jane, her eyes ablaze with newfound strength, confronted the spectral apparitions that manifested around Ms. Hassan. Jacob, his past entwined with the witch's machinations, focused his will to unravel the threads of her influence.

The struggle reached its crescendo as Gal, guided by an inner strength, raised her hand, amulet aglow, and uttered a final incantation. The energies within the amulets surged, resonating with the echoes of the trio's shared journey.

The room convulsed, a tempest of conflicting forces colliding in a spectacular display of magic. Ms. Hassan, her power waning, unleashed a guttural scream that reverberated through the dimensions.

With a blinding flash, the amulets expelled a radiant burst of energy, enveloping Ms. Hassan in a luminescent cocoon. The room quivered, the very fabric of reality warping in response to the cataclysmic clash.

As the brilliance subsided, Gal, Jane, and Jacob stood amidst the remnants of their mystical battle. The once malevolent force that was Ms. Hassan now lay in a weakened state, stripped of her supernatural veneer.

MS. HASSAN

(whispering)

You may have won this round, mortals, but the dance of shadows is eternal.

With those cryptic words, Ms. Hassan dissipated into an ethereal mist, leaving behind only the echoes of her ominous proclamation. The room, once charged with arcane energies, returned to an eerie calm.

Gal, Jane, and Jacob exchanged glances, the weight of their shared ordeal etched in their eyes. The amulets, now inert, bore witness to a chapter in their lives that defied the boundaries of the mundane.

As they stepped out of Ms. Hassan's home, the moonlit night held a serene quietude. The veil between the mystical and the tangible had been drawn back, revealing the interconnected tapestry of their destinies. The witch next door had been vanquished, but the echoes of her malevolence lingered, a reminder of the delicate balance between the seen and the unseen.

The trio, united by a journey that transcended dimensions, faced the unknown future with a resilience forged in the crucible of their shared odyssey. The witch next door was no more, but the shadows of the mystical realms would forever dance on the edges of their reality.

Chapter 2: The Enchantment

Curiosity, like an insatiable flame, flickered within Gal's heart, driving her to unravel the mysteries concealed behind the witch's veiled invitation. The night air hung heavy with secrecy as Gal, cloaked in shadows, tiptoed through the dimly lit streets towards Ms. Hassan's mysterious residence. The moon, a silent witness to clandestine affairs, cast its silvery glow upon the unsuspecting town.

As Gal approached the imposing structure, the air seemed to thicken with an otherworldly energy. The very essence of Ms. Hassan's home pulsated with an enchantment that beckoned the unsuspecting towards the unknown. With each hesitant step, Gal felt the pull of destiny, a force that blurred the boundaries between curiosity and caution.

The creaking gate, an eerie symphony, announced Gal's arrival into the witch's domain. The house, silhouetted against the moonlit sky, exuded an aura of ageless wisdom and arcane secrets. The windows, like watchful eyes, seemed to scrutinize the intruder who dared to venture into the heart of mystery.

Gal hesitated for a moment, her hand hovering over the door as if sensing the dormant magic that lay beyond. A whispered encouragement, a daring thought, and the door swung open with a muted groan, revealing the enigmatic tapestry that awaited within.

The entrance hall, adorned with flickering candles and ancient symbols etched into the floor, emanated an ambient glow that danced with ethereal shadows. Gal treaded cautiously, feeling the floor beneath her pulse with a subtle energy. The air, thick with a heady mixture of incense and ancient knowledge, wrapped around her senses.

A soft murmur reached her ears, drawing her further into the labyrinthine corridors of Ms. Hassan's abode. Following the mysterious melody, Gal found herself descending a spiral staircase that seemed to lead into the very heart of the unknown.

The basement, a subterranean chamber bathed in a spectral glow, greeted Gal as she descended the last step. To her astonishment, Jane and Sue lay unconscious on the cold, stone floor. The flicker of realization ignited in her eyes—Ms. Hassan's invitation had not been exclusive.

The air in the basement crackled with a latent enchantment, an ethereal force that bound the three friends to the whims of the witch. Gal's initial curiosity waned, replaced by a subtle apprehension that lingered like a wisp of fog in the corners of her mind.

As if choreographed by unseen hands, Jane and Sue stirred to consciousness, their eyes reflecting the bewilderment that mirrored Gal's own thoughts. The basement, a peculiar fusion of ancient ritual and modern desolation, seemed to encapsulate the dichotomy of their situation.

Before the trio could comprehend the surreal reality that surrounded them, the air shimmered with a spectral luminescence. Ms. Hassan, her form draped in an otherworldly elegance, materialized amidst the trio like a shadow weaving into existence. Her eyes, twin orbs of arcane knowledge, bore into their souls with an unsettling intensity.

MS. HASSAN

Welcome, my unwitting pawns. It seems curiosity has led you to the threshold of destiny.

Her voice, a melodic cadence that resonated with both allure and menace, wrapped around them like an invisible web. Gal, Jane, and Sue stood entranced, ensnared by the enchantment that pulsed through the very foundations of Ms. Hassan's home.

MS. HASSAN

You seek to save your beloved teacher, Mr. Willoughby. A noble endeavor, my dear Gal. However, the path to salvation is paved with the retrieval of three amulets scattered across dimensions.

The revelation hung in the air, casting a spell that tethered the trio to a fate beyond their understanding. Ms. Hassan, the orchestrator of this mystical odyssey, unfolded the tapestry of their quest with a wicked smile that betrayed the depths of her arcane knowledge.

MS. HASSAN

To grant your deepest desires, you must traverse realms unknown. The first amulet lies shrouded in the echoes of a haunted mansion, a realm where spirits and memories intertwine.

The basement quivered as the boundaries of reality bent to Ms. Hassan's will. With a wave of her hand, the trio found themselves transported to a place that existed at the confluence of the spectral and the corporeal.

Gal, Jane, and Sue materialized in a moonlit graveyard, surrounded by towering tombstones and an air thick with the whispers of the departed. The haunted mansion loomed in the distance, its silhouette a testament to the ethereal challenges awaiting them.

As they ventured towards the mansion, the enchantment of their journey intensified. The air seemed to echo with the mournful wails of unseen spirits, and the moon cast elongated shadows that danced in rhythmic tandem with the trio's heartbeat.

Chapter 2 marked the inception of a journey into the unknown, a journey where the boundaries between the tangible and the fantastical blurred, and Gal's fate became intertwined with the mystical forces that lurked in the shadows. Little did she know that the substitute had set in motion a sequence of events that would redefine not only her understanding of the world but also the very essence of her existence.

The haunted mansion awaited, a realm of phantoms and secrets that would test the limits of their courage and the strength of their friendship.

As Gal, Jane, and Sue approached the looming façade of the haunted mansion, the air thickened with an otherworldly tension. Shadows clung to the walls like spectral guardians, whispering tales of the past and secrets long forgotten. The moon, their only companion in this ethereal journey, cast an eerie glow on the mansion's weathered stones.

The entrance door, seemingly alive with ancient energy, groaned open as if beckoning the trio to step into the realm of phantoms. Hesitating only momentarily, Gal led the way, her heart pounding with a mix of trepidation and curiosity. The mansion's interior unfolded like a tapestry of forgotten memories, each room a chapter in a ghostly saga.

As they delved deeper into the spectral labyrinth, the very walls seemed to come alive with ethereal echoes. Flickering candlelight revealed ghostly apparitions, trapped in a perpetual dance of memories, reliving moments etched into the fabric of the mansion's haunted history. Portraits of long-deceased occupants stared down from the walls, their eyes telling tales of love, betrayal, and tragedy.

In a grand ballroom, they stumbled upon a spectral waltz frozen in time. Transparent couples twirled in elegant harmony, their laughter echoing through the ages. The room pulsed with a bittersweet nostalgia that tugged at the corners of their consciousness.

Sue, ever impulsive, attempted to join the spectral dance, her hand reaching for an unseen partner. But the ghostly figures paid her no mind, lost in the eternal rhythms of their bygone era. The trio pressed on, leaving the ballroom's haunting echoes behind.

Their journey led them through forgotten libraries, hidden passages, and dimly lit corridors where unseen forces seemed to guide their path. The atmosphere, a delicate balance between enchantment and foreboding, heightened their awareness of the unknown.

Finally, in the mansion's long-forgotten attic, they stumbled upon a dusty chest nestled amidst forgotten relics. The chest emitted a subtle hum, as if resonating with the magic that lingered in the air. Gal cautiously opened it, revealing the first amulet—a shimmering pendant imbued with an otherworldly radiance.

As Gal's fingers touched the amulet, a surge of energy coursed through her, connecting her to dimensions unseen. The room quivered, and a spectral figure materialized—a ghostly apparition with hollow eyes that seemed to convey gratitude.

GHOSTLY APPARITION

Thank you for releasing me from the shackles of this haunted realm. Take the amulet and forge your path through the realms that lie ahead.

The amulet, now a conduit between the living and the ethereal, glowed with newfound power. Gal, Jane, and Sue, united by the shared experience, prepared to leave the haunted mansion behind and embrace the unknown challenges awaiting them.

Little did they know that their return would usher in a confrontation with Ms. Hassan, the malevolent force orchestrating this mystical chessboard. The stage was set for a final reckoning—one that would test the limits of friendship, unravel the mysteries of the amulets, and unveil the true nature of the witch next door. The haunted mansion, with its ghostly inhabitants and arcane secrets, had been but the first chapter in a saga that would redefine their destinies.

As Gal, Jane, and Sue emerged from the haunted mansion, the air crackled with an otherworldly energy that seemed to linger in their wake. The moon, now veiled by wisps of spectral mist, cast an eerie glow on their faces. They exchanged glances, each silently acknowledging the surreal turn their lives had taken.

Their journey into the unknown had only just begun, and the enchanted amulet pulsated with a subtle power, a beacon guiding them to the next dimension. With newfound determination, they set their sights on the deserted beach—a realm where the boundary between the living and the undead blurred like the shifting tides.

Transported to the desolate shores of the remote island resort, the trio found themselves amidst the wreckage of a luxury cruise liner, now home to a legion of undead souls. The beach, once a haven of tranquility, echoed with the guttural moans of zombies—former vacationers turned into mindless husks by an insidious curse.

Gal, Jane, and Sue faced the impending onslaught with a mix of fear and resilience. The zombies, clad in tattered vacation attire, stumbled towards them, driven by an insatiable hunger for the living. In the chaos that ensued, Gal brandished the enchanted amulet, its radiance pushing back the encroaching darkness.

The trio fought valiantly, forming an unspoken bond against the undead horde. Jane, with a makeshift weapon in hand, unleashed a flurry of blows, while Sue showcased unexpected marksmanship skills, her accurate shots felling zombies in their tracks.

Amidst the chaos, a ghastly figure emerged—a Zombie Queen adorned with the second amulet. This twisted incarnation of Ms. Hassan, pregnant and grotesque, commanded the undead with a malevolent authority. In a desperate bid to retrieve the amulet, Gal devised a plan, urging Sue to stay behind as a distraction.

SUE

Go! I'll hold them off. Just get that amulet!

With a heavy heart, Gal and Jane raced towards the stranded cruise liner. The vessel, haunted by the echoes of the living turned undead, harbored not only the amulet but also the looming threat of the Zombie Queen.

As they navigated the labyrinthine halls of the ship, the eerie silence was shattered by distant gunshots and Sue's valiant cries. The specter of loss hung heavy, yet Gal and Jane pressed on, determined to honor their friend's sacrifice.

In the belly of the ship, they confronted the Zombie Queen—a grotesque visage of the once-charming Ms. Hassan. The battle was fierce, the air thick with tension as the fate of the amulet teetered on a knife's edge.

With a strategic strike, Jane incapacitated the Zombie Queen, providing Gal with the opportunity to seize the second amulet. However, their triumph was marred by a sinister twist. From the remains of the fallen Zombie Queen, a Zombie Baby emerged, clutching the amulet and skittering away with unnatural speed.

The realization of Sue's sacrifice hit them like a tidal wave. In a solemn moment of mourning, they vowed to carry the memory of their fallen friend with them, the second amulet now a bittersweet memento of their journey.

Little did they know that their return to the mundane world would herald a confrontation with the witch next door, propelling them further into the web of mystical forces that entwined their destinies. The stage was set for a final reckoning—one that would test the limits of friendship, unravel the mysteries of the amulets, and unveil the true nature of Ms. Hassan, the malevolent force orchestrating this mystical chessboard. The deserted beach, with its echoes of both life and undeath, had been but the second chapter in a saga that would redefine their destinies and the very fabric of reality itself.

Chapter 3: Dimension of the Dead

The graveyard, shrouded in an ethereal mist, welcomed Gal, Jane, and Sue as they materialized in the spooky realm of the dead. Tombstones, weathered by time and adorned with moss, whispered tales of long-forgotten souls. The air was thick with an otherworldly chill, and the girls exchanged uneasy glances as they took in their surroundings.

Before they could acclimate to the eerie ambiance, the ground beneath them trembled, and skeletal hands clawed their way out of the graves. Undead skeletons, animated by a spectral force, emerged with a relentless hunger for the living. The trio sprinted through the graveyard, pursued by the clattering bones that echoed in the stillness of the night.

As they approached the imposing facade of the haunted mansion, its timeworn grandeur spoke of a bygone era. The front door creaked open, beckoning them into the labyrinth of spectral secrets that awaited within. Reluctantly, they entered, and the door swung shut behind them with a haunting finality.

The mansion's interior was a tapestry of faded opulence, a silent witness to the tragedies that unfolded within its walls. Portraits of a once-prosperous family adorned the halls, their eyes seemingly following the intruders with an unsettling gaze. Gal, Jane, and Sue pressed on, guided by an unspoken resolve to uncover the mysteries concealed within the mansion's shadowed corridors.

As they explored, they stumbled upon a grand ballroom frozen in time. The ethereal echoes of a long-gone waltz lingered, and ghostly apparitions twirled in a dance that defied the boundaries of mortality. In a moment of spectral interaction, a ghostly figure extended a hand to Gal, inviting her to join the ethereal dance. With trepidation, she accepted, the dance weaving a connection between the living and the dead.

Amidst the ghostly revelry, whispers of the mansion's tragic history reached their ears. The family that once called this place home had succumbed to greed and dark pacts, sealing their fate with a curse that transcended death. Ms. Hassan's lineage, it seemed, was entwined with malevolence that echoed through the ages.

Driven by a shared determination to break the curse and secure the first amulet, the girls delved deeper into the mansion's secrets. A hidden passage revealed a forgotten family crypt, its entrance concealed behind a tapestry depicting the family's unholy alliance with dark forces.

Within the crypt, they discovered the resting place of the cursed family, their final resting places marked by macabre statues and inscriptions recounting their tragic downfall. At the heart of the crypt lay the first amulet, radiating an otherworldly glow. However, the curse lingered, demanding a collective touch to release the amulet's true power.

Gal, Jane, and Sue, standing before the familial mausoleum, reached out to touch the amulet simultaneously. The air crackled with arcane energy as the curse's grip weakened, and the first amulet's power surged through their beings. In that transformative moment, the mansion trembled, and ghostly apparitions dissipated into the aether.

The trio emerged from the mansion, the curse lifted, and the first amulet securely in their possession. Yet, the revelation of Ms. Hassan's malevolent lineage cast a shadow over their triumph. The haunted mansion, with its ghostly inhabitants and arcane secrets, had been but the third chapter in a saga that would redefine their destinies. Little did they know that their return would usher in a confrontation with Ms.

Hassan, the malevolent force orchestrating this mystical chessboard. The stage was set for a final reckoning—one that would test the limits of friendship, unravel the mysteries of the amulets, and unveil the true nature of the witch next door.

As the trio emerged from the haunted mansion, the weight of the lifted curse lingered in the air. The night had grown still, and an otherworldly glow surrounded them, a residual energy from the amulet they now possessed. However, the revelation of Ms. Hassan's sinister lineage weighed heavily on their minds.

Silent shadows danced across the mansion's façade as if whispering secrets of the past. The girls exchanged somber glances, each contemplating the newfound knowledge that Ms. Hassan's dark legacy reached beyond the boundaries of their own world. The implications of their journey were more profound than they could have fathomed.

The moon hung low in the sky, casting an eerie glow on the surroundings. Gal, Jane, and Sue, now bound by a shared destiny, walked away from the haunted mansion. The journey through the dimension of the dead had left an indelible mark on their souls, and the mysteries that unfolded within its walls resonated in the recesses of their minds.

As they approached the boundary between the spectral realm and the unknown, the very fabric of reality seemed to ripple. A familiar vortex materialized before them, its ethereal glow inviting them to step through the veil of dimensions once more. Uncertainty lingered in the air, but the trio, strengthened by their shared experience, stepped forward with determination.

The transition between dimensions was seamless, and they found themselves once again standing in Ms. Hassan's enigmatic home. The basement, the nexus of their mystical journey, awaited them with its ominous stillness. Little did they know that their return marked the beginning of a confrontation with the malevolent force orchestrating this mystical chessboard.

Ms. Hassan, aware of their success in the dimension of the dead, awaited them with a sly smile. The atmosphere crackled with tension as the girls, now armed with the first amulet, faced the true nature of the witch next door. The stage was set for a final reckoning—one that would test the limits of friendship, unravel the mysteries of the amulets, and unveil the depths of Ms. Hassan's malevolence.

In the dimly lit basement, shadows clung to the walls, and the air was charged with a potent blend of anticipation and dread. The chessboard of fate was arranged, and the pieces were poised for a decisive move. The witch next door, her true form concealed beneath a veneer of normalcy, prepared to reveal her dark intentions.

As the confrontation unfolded, the room pulsated with the clash of mystical energies. The first amulet, now a beacon of power, resonated with the unseen forces that bound their destinies together. The trio, unwitting pawns in a supernatural game, stood firm, determined to face the malevolent force that had ensnared them in this web of enchantment.

Little did they know that the dimension of the dead had merely been a prelude to the escalating challenges that awaited them. The haunted mansion, with its ghostly inhabitants and arcane secrets, had been but the third chapter in a saga that would redefine their destinies. The witch next door, unveiled in her true form, would test the strength of their bonds and the resilience of their spirits.

With bated breath and the first amulet clutched in their hands, Gal, Jane, and Sue prepared to confront the malevolent force that lurked in the shadows—a force that had woven their lives into a tapestry of enchantment, beckoning them toward an unknown fate. The stage was set for the final act, and the curtain was about to rise on the next chapter of their extraordinary journey.

Chapter 4: Island of the Undead

The sensation of being torn from one reality and thrust into another had become a disorienting routine for Gal, Jane, and Sue. As the vortex dissipated, they found themselves standing on the desolate sands of a deserted beach, with the distant echoes of crashing waves as the only semblance of normalcy.

The beach stretched endlessly, an isolated sanctuary untouched by the chaos that awaited them. The air was thick with an ominous quiet, broken only by the distant groans of the undead that lurked beyond the horizon. The trio exchanged wary glances, aware that their journey had led them to a place where the line between the living and the dead blurred.

The once serene beach revealed a macabre secret as a luxury cruise liner, now a derelict vessel, ran aground on the shores. The ship's skeletal structure stood as a haunting reminder of a time when it sailed the seas, filled with laughter and revelry. Now, it harbored an army of the undead, their lifeless eyes fixated on the trio as they descended from the vortex.

A sense of urgency enveloped them as the first wave of zombies emerged from the stranded ship. Jane, Gal, and Sue had become unwitting guests on this nightmarish island, where the undead sought to reclaim the living.

Sue, ever courageous, volunteered to stay behind and serve as a distraction for the approaching horde. Armed with a makeshift barricade and a determination that echoed in her eyes, she prepared to face the impending onslaught. Her sacrifice would buy precious time for Jane and Gal to infiltrate the ship and retrieve the second amulet.

As Jane and Gal navigated the eerie corridors of the abandoned cruise liner, the scent of decay and the echoing moans of the undead surrounded them. The ship, once a haven of luxury, had transformed into a labyrinth of death, each corner harboring the unknown.

Their journey led them deeper into the bowels of the ship, where the air grew heavy with the stench of death. The second amulet, a source of unimaginable power, awaited them in the possession of the Zombie Queen—an undead manifestation of Ms. Hassan, grotesque and pregnant with malevolence.

The encounter with the Zombie Queen unfolded in a chamber adorned with tattered remnants of what was once opulence. The amulet dangled from her lifeless neck, casting an eerie glow that danced with the flickering lights. The moment Jane and Gal laid eyes on the horrifying entity, the stakes of their quest heightened.

The Zombie Queen, a ghastly reflection of Ms. Hassan, turned toward them with vacant eyes. Her movements were erratic, a twisted dance that mirrored the chaos of her existence. In her undead state, she clutched the amulet with an unrelenting grip, a key to powers beyond mortal comprehension.

As the confrontation unfolded, Jane and Gal faced not only the relentless horde of zombies that patrolled the ship but also the relentless determination of the Zombie Queen. The amulet, a coveted prize, embodied the essence of their struggle—a battle between the living and the undead, between the forces of good and the malevolence that had ensnared them.

Sue, on the hotel rooftop, gazed down at the approaching horde with a sniper rifle in hand. The rhythmic percussion of gunfire echoed through the night, a symphony of resistance against the encroaching darkness. Her valiant efforts provided a momentary reprieve, a fleeting opportunity for Jane and Gal to face the undead queen head-on.

However, the Zombie Queen, sensing their intrusion, unleashed a guttural growl that echoed through the corridors. The undead responded with heightened aggression, converging on Jane and Gal as they navigated the labyrinthine passages of the ship.

Amid the chaos, Sue, standing against the backdrop of the moonlit night, faced a relentless assault. The horde closed in, their decaying limbs reaching toward her. As the first of the zombies breached her barricade, she held her ground with unwavering resolve.

The ship, now a battleground between the living and the undead, became a crucible of survival. Jane and Gal pressed forward, the second amulet within reach, yet guarded by the monstrous entity that once wore the face of Ms. Hassan.

The climax of the chapter unfolded as Jane and Gal confronted the Zombie Queen in a harrowing showdown. The corridors echoed with the clash of undead limbs, the moans of the approaching horde, and the desperate struggles of the living against an overwhelming tide of death.

In a final, desperate act, Sue took aim at the Zombie Queen from the rooftop, her sniper rifle echoing through the night. The bullet found its mark, piercing the queen's undead heart. Yet, as the Zombie Queen fell, a new horror emerged—a Zombie Baby, born from the remnants of malevolence.

The Zombie Baby, swift and elusive, snatched the amulet and fled into the depths of the ship. Jane and Gal, now faced with an even more formidable adversary, chased the creature through the belly of the vessel. The labyrinthine corridors became a stage for their pursuit, with the amulet dangling precariously from the tiny undead entity.

As Sue succumbed to the relentless assault, the echo of her sacrifice resonated through the ship. The rooftop, once her vantage point, became a battleground of its own. The undead claimed their prize, and the second amulet remained elusive, slipping further into the clutches of the malevolence that pervaded the ship.

The chapter concluded with a poignant realization—a sacrifice made in the face of overwhelming odds, a pursuit that left Jane and Gal on the precipice of despair. The Island of the Undead, with its derelict cruise liner and relentless horde, had become a crucible that tested not only their courage but also the bonds that held them together.

Little did they know that their return would usher in a confrontation with Ms. Hassan, the malevolent force orchestrating this mystical chessboard. The stage was set for a final reckoning—one that would test the limits of friendship, unravel the mysteries of the amulets, and unveil the true nature of the witch next door. The Island of the Undead, with its relentless onslaught and elusive amulets, had been but the fourth chapter in a saga that would redefine their destinies.

As Jane and Gal emerged from the belly of the undead-ridden cruise liner, the weight of their failure pressed upon them like the thick fog that clung to the deserted beach. The Island of the Undead had proven to be a crucible of loss, sacrifice, and relentless adversity, leaving an indelible mark on the journey they had embarked upon.

The distant moans of the undead echoed behind them as they stepped onto the desolate shore, their eyes scanning the horizon for any sign of Sue. The rooftop, where she valiantly stood against the tide of the undead, now seemed like a distant memory—a haunting testament to the price paid in pursuit of the elusive amulet.

The once tranquil beach bore witness to the aftermath of their encounter—the remains of the stranded cruise liner casting eerie shadows in the moonlight. Jane and Gal, still grappling with the reality of Sue's sacrifice, faced the daunting realization that their quest for the amulets had taken an irreversible toll.

The amulet, now held by the elusive Zombie Baby, remained an enigma—a beacon of power that seemed to slip further away with each passing moment. The Island of the Undead had tested their mettle, revealing the fragility of their unity and the relentless nature of the malevolence they sought to overcome.

As they trudged along the desolate beach, the distant silhouette of Ms. Hassan's home beckoned, casting a looming shadow over the horizon. The substitute teacher, whose true nature as a malevolent witch had set this fantastical journey into motion, awaited their return.

The stage was set for the final reckoning—a confrontation that would unveil the true nature of the witch next door. The trials they faced in the haunted mansion and the Island of the Undead had been but preludes to the grand finale—a cosmic chessboard where each move carried consequences beyond their understanding.

The amulets, fragments of mystical power scattered across dimensions, held the key to their deepest desires. Yet, with each retrieval, the price paid in sorrow and sacrifice escalated. The true cost of their pursuit became an echoing refrain in their hearts, a melody of loss and resilience.

The bonds of friendship that had sustained them through the trials of the haunted mansion and the Island of the Undead now faced their sternest test. The mysteries of the amulets, intricately woven into the fabric of their destinies, awaited unraveling. Ms. Hassan, the orchestrator of this mystical chessboard, stood as the final arbiter of their fates.

As Jane and Gal approached the ominous silhouette of Ms. Hassan's home, a chill ran down their spines. The wind whispered tales of ancient curses and forbidden desires, weaving a narrative that transcended the tangible reality of their suburban lives. The journey into the unknown had reached a pivotal juncture—one where the lines between friend and foe blurred, and the destiny of the witch next door intertwined with their own.

The Island of the Undead had been but a prologue to the grand saga that awaited them. Little did they know that their return would herald the final act—a spectacle that would redefine their destinies and lay bare the true nature of the mystical forces that governed their lives.

As Jane and Gal crossed the threshold into the unknown, their hearts pounded in unison. The echoes of the past chapters resonated within them—the haunted mansion, the deserted beach, the sacrifices made in pursuit of the amulets. Now, with the confrontation looming, they steeled themselves for the climax of their otherworldly journey.

The Island of the Undead, with its relentless onslaught and elusive amulets, had been but the fourth chapter in a saga that had thrust them into the heart of cosmic mysteries. The witch next door, a malevolent force orchestrating their destinies, awaited their arrival with a patience borne from centuries of arcane knowledge.

As the door creaked open, revealing the dimly lit interior of Ms. Hassan's home, Jane and Gal stepped into the unknown. The final reckoning beckoned, and the mysteries of the amulets stood poised for revelation. The chessboard of fate was set—the pieces in place for a confrontation that would transcend the boundaries of the known and plunge them into the depths of an otherworldly reality.

Little did they know that their return would usher in a confrontation with Ms. Hassan, the malevolent force orchestrating this mystical chessboard. The stage was set for a final reckoning—one that would test the limits of friendship, unravel the mysteries of the amulets, and unveil the true nature of the witch next door. The Island of the Undead, with its relentless onslaught and elusive amulets, had been but the fourth chapter in a saga that would redefine their destinies.

Chapter 5: Cornfield of Nightmares

The transition to the Cornfield of Nightmares marked a shift in the fabric of their fantastical journey, thrusting Gal, Jane, and Sue into a dimension veiled in eerie cornfields and haunted farms. The air was thick with an otherworldly tension as the girls landed in a realm where the boundary between the tangible and the supernatural blurred into a dreamscape of terror.

As they emerged from the vortex, the oppressive rustling of the corn stalks filled the air, creating an unsettling symphony that resonated with the echoes of unseen horrors. The landscape, bathed in an ethereal glow, stretched endlessly before them, a labyrinth of nightmares waiting to be unraveled.

Their first encounter with this unsettling dimension was none other than Zombie Sue. The sight of their friend, now transformed into a grotesque semblance of her former self, sent shivers down their spines. Yet, there was no time for sentimentality, for the Cornfield of Nightmares had a sinister story to tell—one entwined with the malevolence of Ms. Hassan.

Before they could fully grasp the gravity of the situation, a chainsaw-wielding killer named Sackface emerged from the shadows. The air resonated with the menacing growl of the chainsaw as Sackface descended upon Zombie Sue, decapitating her in a grotesque spectacle of horror. The crimson splatter and the guttural echoes of the chainsaw's roar painted a vivid tableau of the nightmare they had found themselves entangled in.

However, this macabre encounter took an unexpected turn when Sackface, a figure draped in ominous mystery, revealed himself to be Jacob—a missing person from their home dimension. The reunion was a paradox of relief and bewilderment as Jacob, a survivor of Ms. Hassan's malevolence, joined forces with the girls in their quest for Sue and the elusive third amulet.

Together, the trio navigated the eerie cornfields, each rustling stalk a whisper of secrets waiting to be unveiled. The children of the corn, haunting and otherworldly, watched from the shadows with eyes that gleamed like phosphorescent orbs. The atmosphere was laden with the weight of untold tales, and the quest for the third amulet became a precarious dance with the supernatural forces that governed this nightmarish dimension.

As they delved deeper into the labyrinthine expanse of the Cornfield of Nightmares, Gal, Jane, and Jacob faced challenges that transcended the physical realm. The whispers of the corn children guided them, cryptic clues leading them to the elusive third amulet—a fragment of power that held the key to the girls' deepest desires.

The encounters in this haunting dimension became a crucible of fear and determination. The silhouette of Sackface, once a harbinger of dread, now stood as an unlikely ally in their quest. The severed past and the malevolence of Ms. Hassan echoed in the shadows, intertwining with the quest for the amulet like an intricate tapestry of fate.

The cornfields, bathed in an otherworldly glow, became a stage for the unfolding drama of the mystical chessboard. Each step, each rustle of the corn, carried them closer to the elusive amulet and a reckoning that awaited them upon their return. The Cornfield of Nightmares, with its creepy corn children and enigmatic clues, had become the stage for the penultimate act in their cosmic odyssey.

As Gal, Jane, and Jacob reached the heart of the cornfields, a clearing revealed itself—a surreal tableau that seemed frozen in time. The moon cast an eerie glow upon an ancient circle of stones, the ground bearing the scars of arcane rituals. In the center lay the third amulet, radiating an ethereal energy that sent shivers down their spines.

The children of the corn emerged from the shadows, their albino visages a stark contrast to the nightmarish landscape. Their voices, a chorus of whispers, resonated with a cryptic message—the final piece of the puzzle that would complete the amulet and seal their fate.

The ritual commenced, each of them touching the amulet with a sense of trepidation. The vortex, a cosmic whirlwind, materialized before them, promising a return to their home dimension. The Cornfield of Nightmares, with its haunting secrets and spectral inhabitants, faded into the background as they stepped into the vortex.

Little did they know that their return would usher in a confrontation with Ms. Hassan, the malevolent force orchestrating this mystical chessboard. The stage was set for a final reckoning—one that would test the limits of friendship, unravel the mysteries of the amulets, and unveil the true nature of the witch next door. The Cornfield of Nightmares, with its creepy corn children and enigmatic clues, had been but the fifth chapter in a saga that would redefine their destinies.

The vortex released them from its cosmic grip, and Gal, Jane, and Jacob found themselves standing once again in the familiar yet foreboding surroundings of Ms. Hassan's home. The air crackled with an unspoken tension, a prelude to the imminent confrontation that awaited them.

Their gaze shifted to the ominous figure of Ms. Hassan, who awaited them with an air of malevolence that seemed to transcend the boundaries of the mundane. The witch next door had orchestrated their journey through dimensions, manipulating their desires like pieces on a mystical chessboard.

As the trio faced Ms. Hassan, the amulets clutched in their hands, the room pulsated with an energy that transcended the material world. The true nature of their quest unfolded before them—a cosmic struggle between the forces of light and darkness, friendship and betrayal.

Ms. Hassan, her eyes ablaze with an otherworldly intensity, demanded the amulets that held the fragments of power. The stage was set for the final act, a confrontation that would determine the fate of not only the three friends but the very fabric of reality itself.

Gal, Jane, and Jacob exchanged a knowing glance—a silent pact forged through the trials of haunted dimensions and spectral encounters. Their friendship, tested through the crucible of the unknown, stood as a beacon against the encroaching darkness.

With a deceptive smile, Gal handed over the amulets, each fragment pulsating with a cosmic energy that resonated with the untold mysteries of the universe. Ms. Hassan, her fingers brushing against the ancient artifacts, reveled in the culmination of her dark ambitions.

Yet, the trio had devised a cunning ruse. In a daring twist, they revealed a bag, not containing the amulets, but instead harboring the zombified head of Sue—their fallen comrade who had sacrificed herself in the face of the undead onslaught.

A moment of shock and horror contorted Ms. Hassan's features as the zombie head snapped and gnashed its teeth. The curse of the undead, a repercussion of her malevolent deeds, had returned to haunt her. The tables had turned, and the very forces she sought to control now stood as instruments of her demise.

Gal, seizing the opportune moment, shattered the first amulet. The room reverberated with a cacophony of mystical energy as the fragment disintegrated, stripping Ms. Hassan of a portion of her dark power. The malevolence that had defined her existence recoiled, and her form began to twist and deform.

Jane, undeterred by the horror unfolding before her, shattered the second amulet with a resolute strike. The fragments of power dispersed into the ether, leaving Ms. Hassan in a weakened and grotesque state. The once formidable witch now stood vulnerable, stripped of the very essence that had fueled her wicked machinations.

Gal, holding the third and final amulet, paused. The room hung in suspense, the air thick with the remnants of mystical energies. With a determined gaze, Gal swung the amulet downward, its impact resonating with the final revelation.

The third amulet shattered, its cosmic fragments dispersing into the unknown. Ms. Hassan, now a decrepit and powerless figure, succumbed to the consequences of her insatiable thirst for dominion over the mystical forces. The room, once a stage for dark machinations, now bore witness to the aftermath of a cosmic reckoning.

The girls, standing amidst the remnants of shattered amulets and the feeble form of Ms. Hassan, knew that their journey had reached its zenith. The Witch Next Door, once an enigma veiled in shadows, had been unveiled in her true, powerless form.

In a final act of closure, Gal and Jane set ablaze the remnants of Ms. Hassan's home—a symbolic purification that marked the end of a chapter in their lives. The flames licked the air, consuming the vestiges of the mystical chessboard and the haunting secrets it held.

As the embers danced into the night, the trio emerged from the fiery crucible, forever changed by the mystical odyssey that had unfolded. Little did they know that their return, marked by the smoldering ruins of the witch's abode, would usher in a new beginning—one where friendship triumphed over darkness and the true essence of their destinies awaited revelation.

The Witch Next Door, vanquished and powerless, faded into the annals of forgotten nightmares. The trio, with a shared glance of understanding, stepped into the cool night air—a testament to the resilience of friendship in the face of cosmic forces. The saga of Gal, Jane, and Jacob, intertwined with the mystical unknown, had reached its resolution, leaving behind echoes of a journey that defied the boundaries of the tangible and the fantastical.

As the trio emerged from the dissipating shadows of Ms. Hassan's abode, a profound silence settled over the night, broken only by the distant crackling of fading flames. The air, once thick with mystical energies, now bore the scent of extinguished embers and the promise of a new dawn.

Gal, Jane, and Jacob, bound by the unspoken bond forged through the trials of otherworldly dimensions, exchanged a glance that spoke volumes. Their shared understanding transcended the words that lingered unspoken, echoing the resilience of friendship that had withstood the malevolence of cosmic forces.

The cool night air seemed to carry whispers of the saga that had unfolded—the haunting mysteries, the spectral encounters, and the final confrontation that had vanquished the Witch Next Door. The trio, having braved the unknown, now stood at the threshold of a new beginning, their destinies reshaped by the journey that defied the boundaries of the tangible and the fantastical.

As they walked away from the remnants of Ms. Hassan's dwelling, the ruins smoldering behind them, they felt a weight lift from their shoulders. The echoes of the mystical odyssey reverberated in their minds, leaving behind a profound realization—they were not merely survivors but architects of their own destiny.

The saga of Gal, Jane, and Jacob, a tale woven with threads of friendship, courage, and the resilience of the human spirit, reached its resolution beneath the canvas of the night sky. The Witch Next Door, once a malevolent force, now existed only in the annals of forgotten nightmares, a cautionary tale etched in the fabric of their shared history.

With every step they took, the trio embraced the uncertainty of what lay ahead. The cosmic forces that had entangled their fates had, in turn, molded them into individuals whose spirits had been tempered by the fires of otherworldly trials.

Gal, the resilient leader, Jane, the stalwart companion, and Jacob, the unexpected ally, strolled into the cool night air with a sense of purpose—an understanding that the journey through the mystical unknown had not only reshaped their destinies but also fortified the bonds of friendship that transcended the boundaries of the tangible and the fantastical.

The night sky, adorned with stars that bore witness to the cosmic odyssey, seemed to offer a nod of approval. The saga of Gal, Jane, and Jacob may have concluded, but the echoes of their mystical journey resonated in the cosmos—a testament to the enduring power of friendship in the face of the enigmatic and the extraordinary.

Chapter 6: The Children's Clue

The moon hung high in the velvety night sky, casting an ethereal glow over the eerie cornfields that stretched as far as the eye could see. Gal and Jane, having survived the harrowing trials of the haunted mansion, the island of the undead, and the cornfield of nightmares, found themselves standing at the crossroads of their mystical journey.

As they navigated the dimly lit paths between towering cornstalks, the air was thick with an otherworldly energy, and the occasional rustle of leaves seemed to carry whispers from unseen spirits. The children of the corn, guardians of this enigmatic dimension, awaited the arrival of the two seekers entangled in the cosmic tapestry.

Gal and Jane exchanged a glance, their eyes reflecting the shared courage that had brought them this far. The children, with their pale faces and solemn gazes, emerged from the shadows. It was an unsettling sight, yet the duo pressed on, driven by the urgency of their quest.

"Seekers of the amulet," spoke a young boy, his voice carrying a weight beyond his years. "You tread upon the threshold of destiny. The third amulet, a key to unimaginable power, lies hidden, waiting for those with the fortitude to seek its truth."

Gal stepped forward, her determination unyielding. "We need that amulet to end this once and for all. To stop Ms. Hassan."

The children, their expressions unchanged, seemed to share a silent communication. Finally, a girl with hair as golden as the moonlight spoke, "To unravel the amulet's secret, you must face your deepest fears. Only then will the path reveal itself."

As if conjured by the words, the surroundings transformed. The cornfield, once silent, now echoed with haunting whispers and phantom footsteps. Shadows danced on the periphery of their vision, and the air became charged with the manifestations of their fears.

Gal's heart raced as the specter of her estrangement from Jane and Sue materialized before her. The rift that had severed their friendship seemed insurmountable. Jane confronted the specter of her own vulnerability, a fear she had hidden beneath a facade of strength. The children observed, their eyes reflecting an understanding that transcended the confines of their supernatural realm.

With the courage born from necessity, Gal and Jane confronted their fears head-on. They reached out to each other, mending the frayed threads of their friendship that had unraveled in the face of the unknown. The children, their expressions softening, nodded in approval.

"The path is revealed," whispered the golden-haired girl. "Follow it, for your destinies are intertwined with the fate of Ms. Hassan. But heed our warning—do not grant her the power of the amulet, for its consequences are beyond reckoning."

The path unveiled itself, a trail of luminescent flowers leading deeper into the cornfield. Gal and Jane, fortified by the mending of their friendship and armed with the newfound knowledge from the children, ventured forth into the heart of the dimension.

As they walked, the children faded into the shadows, their enigmatic presence echoing in the rustle of leaves and the distant murmurs of the cornfield. The quest for the third amulet had taken a crucial turn, and the duo carried the weight of their intertwined destinies with a sense of purpose.

The luminescent flowers guided them through a maze of towering cornstalks, each step resonating with the anticipation of a final confrontation. The Children's Clue, a pivotal chapter in their mystical journey, had set the stage for the ultimate reckoning—one that would test the limits of friendship and reveal the true nature of the witch next door.

As they delved deeper, the cornfield seemed to stretch endlessly, the luminescent trail weaving a tapestry of light through the labyrinthine passages. Gal and Jane, their eyes fixed on the distant glow, sensed that the culmination of their odyssey drew near.

Unbeknownst to them, the cosmic forces that had guided their journey watched in silent anticipation. The enigmatic dance between seekers and guardians had reached a crescendo, and the true test of their mettle awaited in the shadows of the impending confrontation.

The Children's Clue, a beacon in the cosmic tapestry, had illuminated the path ahead. The duo pressed on, unaware of the challenges that lay in wait and the revelations that would reshape the narrative of their intertwined destinies.

The luminescent trail guided Gal and Jane through the winding corridors of the cornfield, weaving a radiant path that cut through the darkness like a celestial river. The whispers of the cornchildren lingered in the air, a gentle reminder of the otherworldly presence that watched over their quest.

As they walked, the atmosphere grew increasingly charged with an arcane energy. The very air seemed to hum with an otherworldly resonance, and the rustle of the cornstalks carried an ethereal melody. Gal and Jane exchanged glances, their unspoken connection a testament to the bonds forged through the trials of their mystic journey.

The luminescent flowers led them to a clearing bathed in an otherworldly glow. At its center stood a spectral figure, a manifestation of the mystical forces that governed this dimension. The figure beckoned them forward, its voice a soft echo that resonated in the caverns of their consciousness.

"Seekers of the amulet," the spectral figure intoned, "you have faced your fears and mended the fractures of your friendship. Now, the final challenge awaits. Beyond this clearing lies the heart of the dimension, where the third amulet awaits, entwined with the fate of Ms. Hassan."

Gal and Jane nodded in acknowledgment, their determination unwavering. The spectral figure continued, "But beware, for the amulet carries the essence of cosmic power. Its granting must not fall into the hands of Ms. Hassan, for the consequences are vast and unpredictable."

With these cryptic words, the figure dissipated into a shimmering mist, leaving the duo standing at the threshold of the final leg of their quest. The luminescent trail extended beyond the clearing, leading them deeper into the heart of the cornfield.

As they ventured forth, the shadows of the cornfield seemed to come alive with elusive shapes and ethereal whispers. The air pulsated with an anticipatory energy, and the luminescent trail guided them through a surreal dreamscape of shifting perspectives and mystical illusions.

At the culmination of the trail, they arrived at the center of a vast cornfield, where an ancient stone altar stood bathed in an otherworldly glow. Upon the altar rested the third amulet, a crystalline artifact that seemed to capture the very essence of cosmic forces.

Gal and Jane approached the amulet with a mix of trepidation and awe. Its surface shimmered with iridescent hues, revealing glimpses of distant galaxies and unknown dimensions. As they reached out to touch it, a surge of energy coursed through them, intertwining their destinies with the artifact.

The amulet spoke to their souls, revealing fragments of its origin and the purpose for which it was crafted. It was a safeguard against the misuse of cosmic power, a key to balance the forces that governed the mystical realms. In the wrong hands, its granting could unleash cataclysmic events that transcended the boundaries of reality.

Gal and Jane, their minds attuned to the cosmic whispers, understood the gravity of their mission. With the third amulet in their possession, they held the key to Ms. Hassan's defeat and the restoration of cosmic equilibrium. The luminescent trail, having fulfilled its purpose, faded away, leaving them standing at the epicenter of their mystical odyssey.

Unbeknownst to the seekers, the cosmic forces that had guided their journey observed in silent contemplation. The intertwining destinies of Gal, Jane, and the amulets had become a narrative written in the cosmic script, and the final act awaited its unfolding.

As they prepared to leave the cornfield, a portal of swirling energy materialized before them. The luminescent trail, now transformed into a celestial gateway, beckoned them back to their home dimension. The stage was set for the ultimate reckoning, and the echoes of their journey resonated through the mystical tapestry that bound their fates.

Gal and Jane, their hearts pulsating with newfound purpose, stepped through the portal, leaving behind the enigmatic dimension of the cornfield. Little did they know that their return would usher in the final confrontation with Ms. Hassan, the malevolent force orchestrating the cosmic chessboard.

The Children's Clue, the beacon that had illuminated their path, had paved the way for the ultimate reckoning—one that would test the limits of friendship, unravel the mysteries of the amulets, and unveil the true nature of the witch next door. The cosmic forces awaited the resolution of this intricate dance between seekers and destiny, and the saga of Gal and Jane hurtled toward its climactic conclusion.

Gal and Jane emerged from the celestial portal, their surroundings shifting from the eerie cornfields to the familiar sights of their home dimension. The transition left them momentarily disoriented, but the weight of the third amulet in their hands grounded them in the reality of their mission.

As they stepped into the earthly realm, the cosmic forces that had guided their journey lingered, unseen but ever-present. The whispers of the mystical beings echoed through the fabric of reality, an ethereal chorus anticipating the impending confrontation with Ms. Hassan.

The duo found themselves standing on the outskirts of Jefferson High School, where the saga had begun with a seemingly innocuous substitute teacher. The once-familiar halls now held an undercurrent of cosmic tension, and the air buzzed with an energy that transcended the mundane.

With resolute determination, Gal and Jane made their way toward Ms. Hassan's residence. The dark silhouette of the witch's house loomed against the evening sky, a foreboding presence that marked the epicenter of their mystical odyssey.

As they approached the front door, a cold gust of wind swept through the air, carrying with it an eerie whisper. The cosmic forces, ever vigilant, seemed to murmur cryptic assurances, as if guiding the seekers toward their final reckoning.

The door creaked open as they entered the dimly lit foyer. The atmosphere within the house felt charged with an ominous anticipation, and the shadows seemed to dance with malevolent intent. Gal and Jane exchanged glances, their shared resolve unwavering in the face of the impending confrontation.

A voice echoed through the halls, reverberating with a blend of malice and desperation. "You have the amulets," Ms. Hassan's voice rang out, dripping with a sinister undertone. "Now, fulfill your end of the bargain."

The duo advanced further into the house, the third amulet clutched in Gal's hand, resonating with a cosmic pulse. The cosmic forces, aware of the pivotal moment unfolding, guided their steps with an unseen hand.

In the heart of the living room, Ms. Hassan awaited, her eyes aflame with a twisted hunger for power. The amulets lay on the table, shimmering with an ethereal radiance that mirrored the cosmic forces at play.

Gal and Jane, standing firm, exchanged a silent understanding. The final reckoning was at hand. Ms. Hassan, her malevolent gaze fixed on the amulets, extended her hand, demanding the artifacts that held the key to her desires.

But the seekers, fueled by the cosmic revelations and the trials of their journey, had no intention of succumbing to the witch's dark machinations. Gal stepped forward, her voice resonating with a newfound strength.

"We know the consequences," Gal declared, her gaze unwavering. "The amulets won't be used to grant power to the likes of you. The cosmic forces have guided us, and we choose to defy the destiny you sought to impose."

As Ms. Hassan lunged forward, a surge of cosmic energy enveloped the room. The amulets, now conduits of celestial power, resonated with the seekers' defiance. The cosmic forces, no longer silent observers, manifested in a radiant display that defied the boundaries of the tangible and the fantastical.

In an explosive burst of light, the amulets shattered, releasing a cosmic wave that engulfed Ms. Hassan. The malevolent force that had orchestrated the mystical chessboard was rendered powerless, stripped of the cosmic energies she sought to harness.

Gal and Jane, shielded by the celestial energies, watched as Ms. Hassan transformed into a mere mortal. The cosmic forces, satisfied with the seekers' resilience, withdrew into the unseen realms, leaving behind echoes of their enigmatic presence.

The witch next door, vanquished and powerless, faded into the annals of forgotten nightmares. The trio, with a shared glance of understanding, stepped into the cool night air—a testament to the resilience of friendship in the face of cosmic forces.

The saga of Gal, Jane, and Jacob, intertwined with the mystical unknown, had reached its resolution, leaving behind echoes of a journey that defied the boundaries of the tangible and the fantastical. As they exited the once-darkened abode, now free from the shadow of the witch, the cosmic forces whispered their approval, acknowledging the seekers' triumph over destiny.

Little did they know that their return to the ordinary world would be a harbinger of newfound possibilities. The echoes of their journey resonated through the cosmic tapestry, a testament to the enduring spirit of friendship that transcended the boundaries of mortal existence.

The saga of Gal, Jane, and Jacob, with its cosmic twists and ethereal turns, had rewritten the narrative of their destinies. As they stepped into the moonlit night, the mysteries of the amulets and the true nature of the witch next door remained etched in the cosmic memory, a timeless testament to the enduring power of friendship against the forces that lurk in the mystical unknown.

Chapter 7: Return to Reality

As Gal and Jane emerged from the cosmic portal, the transition from the mystical dimensions to the familiar surroundings of their home dimension felt both surreal and grounding. The cosmic forces, having guided them through the labyrinthine journey, seemed to linger in the air—a silent witness to the seekers' return.

The duo found themselves standing in the very heart of the witch's lair, the ominous residence of Ms. Hassan. The atmosphere within the house carried echoes of the recent cosmic confrontation, a residual energy that hinted at the otherworldly events that had transpired.

Their return, however, was not without its challenges. Jacob, their ally in the cosmic odyssey, was conspicuously absent. A sense of urgency gripped them, knowing that their confrontation with Ms. Hassan was inevitable.

The living room, once a stage for cosmic reckoning, now bore witness to a more terrestrial showdown. Ms. Hassan, the malevolent force orchestrating the mystical chessboard, awaited their arrival with a sinister calmness.

"I see you've returned," Ms. Hassan's voice echoed through the room, a mixture of disdain and anticipation. "The amulets, if you please. Time is of the essence."

Gal and Jane exchanged a glance, a silent understanding passing between them. The cosmic forces that had guided their journey had not abandoned them. The seekers stood united, resolved to confront the witch next door and put an end to her dark reign.

Gal, holding the remnants of the shattered amulets, faced Ms. Hassan with a steely gaze. "We've come to put an end to this," she declared, her voice resonating with determination.

Ms. Hassan's eyes gleamed with a malevolent glint. "You cannot defy destiny, my dear. The cosmic forces may have guided you, but their power wanes in the face of my desires."

In a calculated move, Gal opened a bag she had been carrying, revealing the preserved head of Zombie Sue. The decaying visage seemed to sneer at Ms. Hassan, a grotesque reminder of the cosmic journey's toll.

Jane, standing by Gal's side, confronted Ms. Hassan. "Your reign ends here. We won't allow you to use the amulets for your twisted purposes."

Ms. Hassan, sensing a defiance that echoed the cosmic forces' intervention, extended her hand to claim the remnants of the amulets. But the seekers were prepared for this moment—a moment that would mark the final confrontation between mortals and the mystical unknown.

As Gal handed over the bag, a triumphant glint flashed in Ms. Hassan's eyes. However, the contents of the bag were not what the witch expected. Instead of the intact amulets, she found Zombie Sue's head, preserved in a grotesque display.

Before Ms. Hassan could react, Zombie Sue's decaying mouth snapped shut, delivering a fatal bite. The cosmic energies that had once been harnessed by the amulets now coursed through Zombie Sue's remains, transforming Ms. Hassan into a vessel of the very darkness she sought to control.

The witch convulsed, a grotesque fusion of mortal and supernatural forces. The seekers, witnessing the demise of the malevolent force, stood firm in their resolve. Gal and Jane, their eyes reflecting a mixture of relief and triumph, stepped back as the cosmic energies consumed Ms. Hassan.

With a final howl, Ms. Hassan collapsed to the floor, her reign of darkness extinguished. The cosmic forces, having fulfilled their purpose, retreated into the unseen realms, leaving behind the mundane remnants of the once-confronted witch.

Realizing that the source of the dark power had been vanquished, Gal and Jane wasted no time. Their actions, guided by a cosmic dance beyond mortal comprehension, carried a poetic justice that echoed through the very fabric of reality.

Together, they doused the house with accelerants, ensuring that the remnants of Ms. Hassan's dark reign would be purged in the cleansing flames. The cosmic portal that had bridged the mystical dimensions with their home dimension shimmered one last time before dissipating into the cosmic tapestry.

As the flames consumed the house, the ethereal echoes of their journey resonated in the night air. The saga of Gal, Jane, and Jacob, marked by the cosmic forces that defied the boundaries of the tangible and the fantastical, had reached its conclusion.

The darkened abode that had once harbored the malevolent force now crumbled under the cosmic retribution. The flames danced in a mesmerizing display, casting shadows that seemed to whisper the secrets of the mystical unknown.

Gal and Jane, standing outside the conflagration, watched as the last vestiges of Ms. Hassan's dark magic were engulfed by the cleansing fire. The cosmic forces, having orchestrated their journey, faded into the cosmic tapestry, leaving behind a sense of closure and the promise of newfound possibilities.

The saga of the witch next door, with its cosmic twists and ethereal turns, had come to an end. The seekers, their destinies forever intertwined with the mystical unknown, embraced the cool night air—a testament to the enduring spirit of friendship that transcended mortal existence.

Little did they know that their return to the ordinary world would be a rebirth of sorts. The echoes of their journey resonated through the cosmic tapestry, a timeless testament to the enduring power of friendship against the forces that lurked in the mystical unknown.

In the aftermath of the fiery reckoning, Gal and Jane stood amidst the lingering embers, their eyes reflecting the transformative journey that had unfolded. The ordinary world, once overshadowed by the mystical unknown, now awaited them with a renewed sense of possibilities.

The cosmic echoes of their odyssey resonated through the tapestry of existence, intertwining with the fabric of reality. The bonds of friendship, tested and strengthened in the crucible of cosmic forces, had emerged unbroken—a testament to the enduring power of camaraderie against the unseen forces that lurked in the shadows.

As the remnants of Ms. Hassan's dark reign crumbled in the cleansing flames, a sense of liberation enveloped Gal and Jane. The witch next door, once a malevolent force manipulating the threads of destiny, now existed only as a whisper in the cosmic winds.

The cosmic portal, the ephemeral bridge between dimensions, had dissipated into the unseen realms. Its closure marked the conclusion of a saga that had defied the boundaries of the tangible and the fantastical. Gal and Jane, standing on the precipice of the ordinary, carried within them the echoes of a journey that transcended mortal understanding.

The night air, cool and refreshing, seemed to carry whispers of the mystical unknown. The cosmic forces, having played their part in the seekers' quest, now retreated into the unseen corners of the cosmos, leaving behind a world reborn from the ashes of cosmic confrontation.

Amidst the ruins of Ms. Hassan's house, the cosmic tapestry echoed with a timeless truth—the enduring power of friendship against the forces that lurked in the mystical unknown. Gal and Jane, their destinies forever intertwined, shared a glance of understanding, acknowledging the profound impact of their shared journey.

The echoes of the cosmic forces reverberated through the ordinary world, a silent reminder of the unseen battles fought and the cosmic dance that had guided their steps. Little did they know that their return to the ordinary world was not just a conclusion but a rebirth—a rebirth of friendships, of understanding, and of a newfound appreciation for the mysteries that lingered beneath the surface of reality.

The next morning, as the sun cast its golden hues over the town, Gal and Jane found themselves standing on the familiar streets. The scars of their cosmic odyssey were hidden beneath the veneer of the mundane, but the echoes persisted—an indelible mark on the canvas of their lives.

Gal's father, unaware of the cosmic battles fought and won, greeted her with a warm smile. Life in the ordinary world resumed its course, but the experiences of the mystical unknown had left an imprint on Gal and Jane that transcended the mundane.

The saga of the witch next door, with its cosmic twists and ethereal turns, had become a chapter in the book of their lives—a chapter that would be revisited in quiet moments and shared glances. The cosmic forces, having guided their journey, now allowed them the freedom to navigate the ordinary world on their own terms.

As the days passed, Gal and Jane rekindled their friendship with a newfound appreciation for the bonds that held them together. The town, once overshadowed by the witch's dark presence, now embraced them with a sense of familiarity.

Unbeknownst to them, a familiar face emerged on the horizon. Jacob, the missing person from their home dimension, approached with a wry smile. His survival in the cosmic vortex had led him back to the ordinary world, and the trio found themselves reunited.

"We've got a lot of catching up to do," Jacob remarked, his eyes reflecting the resilience forged in the crucible of the cosmic unknown.

Gal, Jane, and Jacob, their destinies forever intertwined, embarked on a new chapter—a chapter that unfolded in the ordinary world but carried with it the echoes of the mystical unknown. The town, once shrouded in cosmic mysteries, became the backdrop for their shared adventures.

Little did they know that the cosmic forces, having played their part in the saga of the witch next door, continued to weave the unseen threads of destiny. The echoes of their journey resonated through the cosmic tapestry, a timeless testament to the enduring power of friendship against the forces that lurked in the mystical unknown.

And so, under the ordinary sky, amidst the familiar streets, the trio stepped into the next chapter of their lives—a testament to the resilience of friendship, the mysteries that lingered in the cosmic corners, and the enduring spirit that transcended the boundaries of the tangible and the fantastical.

As the trio ventured into the next chapter of their lives, the ordinary town embraced them with open arms. Gal, Jane, and Jacob navigated the familiar streets, each step resonating with the echoes of their extraordinary journey. The town, once haunted by the malevolent force of the witch next door, now bore witness to the resilience of friendship and the indomitable spirit that transcended cosmic boundaries.

The ordinary days unfolded, punctuated by shared laughter, quiet contemplations, and the unspoken understanding that their destinies had been forever altered by the mystical unknown. Gal's father, though oblivious to the cosmic battles fought, witnessed the rekindling of his daughter's bond with Jane and the arrival of Jacob with a warm heart.

The trio explored the ordinary world with a newfound appreciation, recognizing the beauty in the mundane and the mysteries that lingered beneath the surface of the everyday. The scars of their cosmic odyssey remained hidden, visible only in the shared glances and unspoken words that communicated volumes about their shared experiences.

In the quiet moments, as the sun dipped below the horizon and the ordinary sky painted itself with hues of twilight, Gal, Jane, and Jacob gathered at their favorite spot—a place where their friendship had once blossomed. The cosmic echoes, though silent, lingered, creating an invisible thread that bound them together.

The ordinary world became a canvas for their shared adventures, filled with road trips, laughter-filled nights, and the kind of camaraderie that only emerges from overcoming extraordinary challenges. Little did they know that their journey had not just concluded; it had merely transformed into a new phase—one where the cosmic forces continued to weave unseen threads in the tapestry of their lives.

As the seasons changed and the town embraced the ebb and flow of life, Gal, Jane, and Jacob discovered that the enduring power of friendship was not confined to the mystical unknown. It was a force that breathed life into their ordinary days, infusing each moment with a sense of magic that transcended the boundaries of the tangible and the fantastical.

The echoes of the witch next door, vanquished and powerless, faded into the annals of forgotten nightmares. The trio, with a shared glance of understanding, stepped into the cool night air—a testament to the resilience of friendship in the face of cosmic forces. The saga of Gal, Jane, and Jacob, intertwined with the mystical unknown, had reached its resolution, leaving behind echoes of a journey that defied the boundaries of the tangible and the fantastical.

And so, under the ordinary sky, amidst the familiar streets, the trio embraced the uncertainties of the future, fortified by the lessons learned in the cosmic dance. The ordinary world, once a backdrop to their cosmic odyssey, now unfolded as a stage for the enduring bonds of friendship—a friendship that had withstood the tests of mystical realms and emerged unscathed.

As they walked into the next chapter of their lives, the cosmic forces, having played their part in the saga, watched from the unseen corners, acknowledging the indomitable spirit of friendship that had prevailed against the forces that lurked in the mystical unknown. The echoes of their journey resonated through the cosmic tapestry, leaving an imprint on the unseen realms—a testament to the enduring power of camaraderie that defied the boundaries of ordinary and extraordinary.

Chapter 8: Life After the Witch

In the aftermath of the cosmic ordeal, life gradually settled into a semblance of normalcy for Gal and Jane. The echoes of their mystical journey lingered, shaping their perspectives and intertwining their destinies in ways they could hardly fathom. The town, once plagued by the malevolent force of the witch next door, embraced the ordinary days with a newfound sense of tranquility.

Gal and Jane, now inseparable, devoted their time to rebuilding the friendship that had weathered the storms of otherworldly challenges. The scars from their cosmic odyssey remained, but instead of being burdens, they became symbols of resilience and shared triumphs. Together, they navigated the hallways of Jefferson High School, once again finding solace in the ordinary rhythms of teenage life.

It was during this time that a surprising revelation unfolded — Jacob, the missing person from their home dimension, had not only survived the vortex but had found his way back to the ordinary world. The trio, fueled by the camaraderie forged in the crucible of cosmic battles, felt a shared sense of purpose and adventure calling to them.

With the school year coming to an end, and the promise of summer hanging in the air, Gal, Jane, and Jacob hatched a plan that would further cement their bond and offer a reprieve from the ordinary. The decision was made: they would spend the summer hunting witches, venturing into the unknown with a shared sense of anticipation.

Jacob's pickup truck, weathered from the miles it had already seen, became their vessel for new adventures. Packed with essentials, a map of potential witch sightings, and a sense of excitement that permeated the air, the trio embarked on a road trip that would take them beyond the familiar boundaries of their town. The ordinary streets gave way to open roads, stretching like ribbons into landscapes unknown.

Their first destination led them to a small town on the outskirts, rumored to be haunted by mystical occurrences. The trio, armed with the lessons learned from their previous encounters, approached the challenges with a blend of caution and curiosity. Each encounter with purported witches unfolded as a puzzle waiting to be solved, a chapter in their ongoing saga that had transcended the limits of the ordinary.

As they journeyed through quaint towns and expansive landscapes, the trio discovered that the mystical forces they sought were not confined to the witch next door's realm. Instead, pockets of the supernatural manifested in various forms—be it cryptic legends, haunted locales, or enigmatic figures hidden in the shadows.

Their road trip unfolded as a montage of eerie encounters, shared laughter under starlit skies, and moments of quiet reflection as the pickup truck carried them through landscapes that blurred the boundaries between the tangible and the fantastical. Jacob, once a missing person lost in the cosmic dance, found a sense of purpose and belonging within the trio.

In their pursuit of witches, they encountered benevolent spirits, ancient artifacts, and clues that hinted at the intricate tapestry connecting the mystical realms. Each chapter of their summer adventure revealed a new layer to the cosmic forces that shaped their destinies, reinforcing the idea that the boundaries between the ordinary and the extraordinary were permeable.

As the summer days unfolded, Gal, Jane, and Jacob found themselves not only hunters of witches but also seekers of truths that transcended the mortal realm. The journey became a testament to the enduring power of friendship, the resilience of the human spirit, and the mysteries that unfolded when one dared to venture beyond the confines of the expected.

And so, under the vast expanse of the summer sky, the trio continued their road trip, chasing the unknown with a shared sense of purpose. Life after the witch became a vibrant tapestry woven with threads of ordinary and extraordinary, a testament to the enduring spirit that defied the limits of what was deemed possible.

As the pickup truck rolled along the open roads, the echoes of their laughter, the whispers of mystical encounters, and the shared glances of understanding resonated through the cosmic tapestry. The ordinary world had become a canvas for extraordinary adventures, and the saga of Gal, Jane, and Jacob continued, leaving an indelible mark on the unseen realms that watched their journey unfold.

In the heart of their summer road trip, the trio found themselves drawn to a town shrouded in an air of mystery. Whispers of an ancient curse, a haunted forest, and a reclusive figure with elusive powers had piqued their curiosity. Gal, Jane, and Jacob navigated the winding roads, guided by the cryptic clues that hinted at a confrontation with forces beyond their previous encounters.

The town, seemingly frozen in time, greeted them with creaking signposts and dilapidated houses that whispered of untold secrets. The trio, undeterred by the ominous aura, delved into the heart of the mystery, seeking the elusive witch who supposedly held dominion over the town's supernatural occurrences.

Their journey led them to a foreboding forest, where shadows danced among ancient trees, and a palpable sense of otherworldly energy hung in the air. As they ventured deeper, the foliage closed in, creating an otherworldly canopy that blocked out the sunlight. Strange symbols marked the trees, hinting at a language older than time itself.

It wasn't long before the trio encountered the guardian of the forest—a spectral figure with eyes that seemed to hold the wisdom of centuries. The guardian, recognizing the cosmic echoes resonating within the seekers, spoke in riddles, revealing fragments of the town's cursed history and the source of the mystical disturbances.

To lift the curse that bound the town, Gal, Jane, and Jacob needed to unravel a series of trials scattered across the haunted landscape. Each trial brought them face to face with manifestations of their deepest fears, forcing them to confront the shadows that lurked within their souls. The forest, with its twisting paths and ethereal illusions, became a crucible of self-discovery.

As they navigated the trials, the trio unearthed the tragic tale of a witch wrongly accused and cursed by the townspeople in a bygone era. The echoes of her anguish resonated through the ghostly apparitions that materialized, each trial a testament to the enduring consequences of unchecked fear.

The final trial revealed the heart of the curse—a relic hidden deep within the forest that bound the witch's spirit to the town. Gal, Jane, and Jacob, guided by the lessons learned from their previous odysseys, braved the labyrinthine depths of the haunted woods to retrieve the relic.

As they approached the sacred site, the air crackled with energy, and the ethereal presence of the witch materialized. Instead of hostility, her eyes bore a mix of sorrow and gratitude. The seekers had become instruments of redemption, lifting the curse that had plagued her for centuries.

With the relic in their possession, the trio returned to the town center. The cosmic forces, once bound by the curse, seemed to sigh in relief. The townspeople, unaware of the supernatural struggles that had unfolded, experienced an unexpected calm as the long-standing curse lifted its grip.

The guardian of the forest, appearing one last time, acknowledged the seekers' resilience. Gal, Jane, and Jacob, having untangled the threads of destiny once more, continued their journey. The pickup truck rolled away from the town, leaving behind a community that would forever be touched by the unseen forces the trio had confronted.

The echoes of their laughter, the whispers of the guardian's wisdom, and the shared glances of understanding resonated through the cosmic tapestry. The ordinary world, once entwined with extraordinary adventures, bore witness to the enduring spirit that transcended the boundaries of the tangible and the fantastical.

And so, as the pickup truck disappeared into the horizon, the saga of Gal, Jane, and Jacob continued—an indomitable force in the cosmic dance between seekers and destiny. The road stretched before them, a symbol of limitless possibilities, as they embraced the unknown with a shared sense of purpose and the enduring power of friendship.

The open road stretched ahead like an uncharted canvas, painted with the hues of twilight. The trio—Gal, Jane, and Jacob—rode into the fading sunlight, leaving the mysteries of the town behind. The echoes of their laughter intertwined with the whispers of the cosmic forces that had guided them through realms unseen.

As the pickup truck carried them toward the vanishing sun, a shared sense of purpose anchored them in the present while the promise of limitless possibilities beckoned from the horizon. The cosmic dance between seekers and destiny continued, and the road became a metaphor for the winding paths of life, an ever-unfolding journey where each twist and turn held the potential for new adventures.

In the gentle hum of the engine and the rhythmic rumble of tires against the asphalt, the trio found solace. Their camaraderie, forged through trials that transcended the ordinary, became a resilient force against the unknown. The enduring power of friendship manifested in the unspoken understanding that bound them together—a silent pact to face whatever cosmic tapestry awaited them.

As the truck traversed through landscapes both mundane and mystical, the trio shared stories of their past adventures and dreams of future conquests. Gal, with her unwavering determination; Jane, fueled by a curiosity that defied the boundaries of the mundane; and Jacob, marked by the scars of battles against malevolent forces—they were a testament to the strength found in companionship.

The stars began to emerge, scattered like celestial breadcrumbs in the vast canvas of the night sky. A cosmic symphony played overhead, a silent ode to the interconnectedness of all things. The road, now illuminated by the truck's headlights, seemed to disappear into the shadows, leaving the destination shrouded in mystery.

Their journey was more than a physical passage through landscapes; it was a metaphorical exploration of the human spirit, a quest for understanding the enigmatic forces that shaped destinies. The truck became a vessel for stories, a mobile haven where friendships were forged, and destinies interwove with the unseen threads of the cosmos.

As the trio ventured into the night, the road became a bridge between realms—between the known and the unknown, the tangible and the fantastical. In each passing mile, the echoes of their laughter resonated with the cosmic forces, creating an ethereal harmony that transcended the confines of the pickup truck.

And so, under the canopy of stars, amidst the rhythmic hum of the engine and the whispered secrets of the night, the saga of Gal, Jane, and Jacob unfolded. The road, with its twists and turns, ascents and descents, mirrored the ebb and flow of life's complexities.

As the truck carried them toward new horizons, the trio embraced the unknown with open hearts. For in the cosmic dance between seekers and destiny, they had become architects of their own narratives, authors of a saga that defied the boundaries of the tangible and the fantastical.

The truck, a vessel of shared dreams and unspoken bonds, ventured into the night, leaving behind the town, the haunted mansion, the island of the undead, the cornfield of nightmares, and the witch next door. The road stretched before them—an invitation to explore the mysteries that awaited beyond the horizon.

As the pickup truck faded into the distance, the cosmic forces whispered their approval. The saga continued, a timeless dance in the grand tapestry of existence, where the enduring power of friendship illuminated the darkest corners of the mystical unknown.

Chapter 9: A Hunter's Pact

The summer sun bathed the trio—Gal, Jane, and Jacob—in a warm embrace as they stood in the quiet haven of Gal's backyard. The remnants of their recent adventures lingered like echoes in the air, a testament to the cosmic forces that had guided them through the mystical unknown. Unbeknownst to them, a new chapter was about to unfold under the brilliant canvas of the summer sky.

Gal, her determination etched in the lines of her expression, gathered the group with an unspoken purpose. Jane, fueled by an insatiable curiosity, and Jacob, bearing the scars of encounters with malevolent forces, shared a silent understanding. The trio, bound by the enduring power of friendship, was ready for the next chapter in their saga.

In the dappled sunlight, Gal unveiled a collection of ancient texts, dusty grimoires, and weathered maps. These artifacts, remnants of a forgotten past, were a treasure trove of knowledge gleaned from their harrowing experiences. Each page whispered secrets, offering clues to the existence of malevolent witches haunting realms beyond their dimension.

Jane, with her keen intellect and thirst for knowledge, sifted through the ancient texts. Her eyes sparkled with excitement as she uncovered cryptic passages, forgotten incantations, and tales of witches who existed at the crossroads of reality. The summer breeze carried the scent of adventure, and Jane's curiosity became a beacon that illuminated the path ahead.

Jacob, his gaze steely and resolute, drew on his experiences from the witch-infested dimensions they had traversed. His missing person status in their home dimension had transformed into a cloak of invisibility in the mystical realms. Armed with insights gained from survival, Jacob became an invaluable guide in their quest to hunt down the malevolent entities that lurked in the shadows.

As the trio delved into the labyrinthine world of folklore, they discovered patterns, recurring motifs, and ancient rituals that hinted at the presence of supernatural forces. Gal, Jane, and Jacob were no longer mere protagonists in a cosmic drama but had become hunters—seekers of truths that eluded the ordinary gaze.

Their unspoken pact materialized like an invisible thread, binding them to a shared purpose. The summer became a season of preparation, a time to equip themselves with knowledge, weapons, and the unyielding determination to confront the malevolent witches that haunted the realms beyond.

Gal, her gaze fixed on the horizon, revealed the first clue—a cryptic message from an ancient scroll that hinted at a witch's lair concealed within the depths of an enchanted forest. Jane's eyes widened with excitement as she deciphered the message, her mind already racing ahead to the mysteries waiting to be unraveled.

Jacob, tracing his fingers over the map, identified potential ley lines and convergence points where the mystical energies converged. These were the crossroads, the thin veils between dimensions where malevolent witches could slip through and wreak havoc. Armed with this knowledge, the trio outlined their journey, plotting a course through realms both familiar and fantastical.

The sun dipped low in the sky, casting long shadows across the backyard—a symbolic transition into the unknown. The trio, now clad in a hunter's resolve, exchanged glances that spoke volumes. Their journey, once dictated by the whims of cosmic forces, had evolved into a purposeful pursuit—a hunter's pact forged under the summer sun.

In the quiet hours of dusk, as fireflies danced in the fading light, the trio gathered around a makeshift table adorned with maps, artifacts, and the echoes of their shared past. Gal, her voice steady, outlined the plan—each step meticulously designed to unravel the mysteries that awaited them.

The first chapter of their new quest was about to unfold—the enchanted forest beckoned, its secrets concealed within the rustling leaves and ancient whispers. The trio, armed with knowledge, friendship, and an unspoken pact, embarked on a journey that would test the limits of their courage and the strength of their bonds.

Under the summer stars, Gal, Jane, and Jacob stood at the threshold of the enchanted forest—a realm where malevolent witches awaited their arrival. The cosmic dance between seekers and destiny continued, and the trio, now hunters in the mystical unknown, stepped into the shadows with a shared sense of purpose.

As the darkness enveloped them, the echoes of their laughter, the whispers of ancient scrolls, and the resonance of their unspoken pact resonated through the cosmic tapestry. The summer night became a canvas for a new chapter—one that would redefine their destinies, challenge the boundaries of the tangible and the fantastical, and unveil the true nature of the hunters they had become.

And so, under the summer stars, the saga of Gal, Jane, and Jacob continued—a relentless force in the cosmic dance between seekers and destiny. The enchanted forest, with its mysteries and malevolent entities, had become the stage for their next supernatural challenge. The hunter's pact held firm, and the trio pressed forward, ready to confront the unknown that lurked in the heart of the enchanted realm.

As the trio ventured into the heart of the enchanted forest, the air thickened with an otherworldly energy. Ancient trees, their gnarled branches reaching for the heavens, cast elongated shadows that seemed to dance to an unseen rhythm. Moonlight filtered through the dense canopy, illuminating the path ahead with an ethereal glow.

Gal, Jane, and Jacob moved in unison, their footsteps synchronized with the pulse of the mystical realm. The enchanted forest, a living tapestry of whispers and ancient secrets, responded to their presence. Birds sang haunting melodies, and the rustle of leaves seemed to convey messages from unseen entities.

Their journey through the labyrinthine trails led them deeper into the heart of the forest. Strange flora, luminescent in the moonlight, adorned the forest floor, creating an otherworldly tableau. The trio, guided by the hunter's pact and a shared sense of purpose, navigated the twists and turns with a determination that echoed through the cosmic tapestry.

As they progressed, the atmosphere became charged with an anticipatory energy. A subtle hum, like the collective breath of the enchanted realm, surrounded them. Gal, attuned to the mystical forces that once shaped their destinies, sensed a convergence point—a place where the fabric between dimensions thinned.

Jane, her eyes gleaming with curiosity, consulted the ancient scroll for guidance. The cryptic symbols seemed to rearrange themselves, forming a coherent map of the enchanted forest. The hunter's pact had led them to this juncture, and the next revelation awaited at the convergence point.

A clearing emerged ahead—a sacred space where moonlight bathed an ancient altar adorned with symbols of forgotten lore. The air seemed to shimmer with energy, and Gal felt a familiar pull—a resonance that hinted at the presence of malevolent forces lurking in the shadows.

As they approached the altar, a spectral figure materialized—a guardian of the enchanted realm. The entity, cloaked in moonlight, spoke in an ancient tongue that resonated through their beings. It warned of the malevolent witch that had ensnared the forest in a web of dark magic, corrupting the very essence of the mystical realm.

Gal, Jane, and Jacob listened intently, their understanding of the cosmic dance between seekers and destiny deepening. The enchanted forest, once a serene sanctuary, now faced a malevolent threat that demanded their intervention. The trio, bound by the hunter's pact, pledged to confront the malevolent witch and free the forest from its sinister grasp.

Guided by the spectral guardian, the trio embarked on a quest within the enchanted forest. The trees whispered ancient incantations, revealing hidden paths and arcane secrets. Strange creatures, guardians of the mystical realm, tested their resolve, and the trio faced challenges that pushed the limits of their courage.

As they journeyed deeper, the malevolent presence grew stronger. The air crackled with dark magic, and the once-vibrant flora withered under the witch's influence. The cosmic forces observed their every move, weaving a narrative that intertwined seekers, destiny, and the impending confrontation with the malevolent entity.

At the heart of the enchanted forest, amidst the twisted roots of an ancient tree, they found the lair of the malevolent witch. The air pulsed with malevolence, and the forest itself seemed to recoil from the dark energy that emanated from the witch's lair.

Gal, Jane, and Jacob stood before the entrance, their resolve unwavering. The hunter's pact, forged under the summer sun, fueled their determination. The stage was set for a final reckoning—one that would test the limits of friendship, unravel the mysteries of the malevolent witch, and unveil the true nature of the supernatural forces that governed their intertwined destinies.

With a shared glance of understanding, the trio entered the lair, stepping into the shadows that concealed the malevolent witch. The cosmic dance between seekers and destiny reached its zenith, and the saga of Gal, Jane, and Jacob continued—a relentless force in the enchanted realm, ready to confront the unknown that awaited them within the heart of darkness.

The lair of the malevolent witch unfurled before them, a realm woven from the fabric of nightmares. Shadows danced on the walls, and an eerie silence hung in the air. The trio moved cautiously, guided by the spectral guardian's warnings and the pulsating energy that emanated from the heart of darkness.

As they ventured deeper into the lair, arcane symbols adorned the walls, pulsing with an ominous glow. The malevolent witch, a master of dark arts, had etched her presence into the very essence of the enchanted realm. The air crackled with anticipation, and the trio knew that their journey had reached a critical juncture.

A voice echoed through the darkness, the malevolent witch's taunts reverberating like whispers of malevolence. "Welcome, seekers," she hissed, her presence materializing before them in a swirl of shadows. Eyes gleaming with ancient knowledge, she surveyed her intruders with a malevolent delight.

Gal, Jane, and Jacob stood firm, their hunter's pact a shield against the dark forces that sought to ensnare them. The malevolent witch, her form shifting between shadows, unleashed tendrils of dark magic that snaked through the air. The cosmic dance between seekers and destiny intensified, each movement propelling them closer to the heart of the confrontation.

In the midst of the arcane battle, Jane consulted the ancient scroll, its symbols now rearranging themselves in response to the malevolent energy. A revelation dawned—a vulnerability within the witch's dark fortress, a nexus of power that could be exploited to break the malevolent grip on the enchanted realm.

With a shared nod, the trio embarked on a perilous journey through the shifting corridors of the lair. The malevolent witch, sensing their intentions, unleashed spectral guardians and illusions to thwart their progress. Yet, the unspoken understanding among Gal, Jane, and Jacob fueled their determination, guiding them through the labyrinth of shadows.

As they approached the nexus of power, the malevolent forces intensified. Whispers of doubt and fear crept into their minds, but the trio's shared resolve remained unbroken. With a synchronized effort, they reached the nexus—a pulsating core of dark energy that fueled the malevolent witch's influence.

Gal, drawing upon the strength forged through previous encounters, channeled her latent abilities. Jane, deciphering the ancient symbols, unleashed a counter-incantation that disrupted the dark magic. Jacob, wielding knowledge gained from his own harrowing experience, struck at the vulnerable points of the witch's defenses.

The enchanted realm trembled as the cosmic forces witnessed the pivotal moment. The malevolent witch, her power waning, unleashed a final surge of dark energy. The trio, bathed in the glow of their shared purpose, stood resilient against the onslaught.

In an explosion of ethereal light, the nexus shattered, dispersing the malevolent forces that gripped the enchanted forest. The lair crumbled, shadows retreating into the cosmic tapestry. The malevolent witch, stripped of her dark power, faded into the echoes of forgotten nightmares.

With a collective breath, Gal, Jane, and Jacob emerged from the crumbling lair, stepping into the moonlit clearing of the enchanted forest. The cosmic dance between seekers and destiny reached its crescendo, leaving behind a transformed realm—a sanctuary restored to its former glory.

The spectral guardian appeared, its form radiating gratitude. The saga of Gal, Jane, and Jacob had not only vanquished a malevolent force but had become an indomitable force in the cosmic dance of the enchanted realm. The trio, bathed in the moonlight of their shared victory, exchanged glances of understanding.

And so, beneath the canopy of the enchanted forest, the trio embraced—their friendship an enduring testament to the resilience of seekers against the forces that lurked in the mystical unknown. The cosmic tapestry, forever altered by their journey, bore witness to the saga of Gal, Jane, and Jacob—a story that transcended the boundaries of the tangible and the fantastical, echoing through the unseen realms that watched their triumphant return.

Chapter 10: The Whispering Woods

The Whispering Woods beckoned, its ancient trees standing tall and proud, their gnarled branches creating a natural tapestry that seemed to breathe with the echoes of centuries gone by. Gal, Jane, and Jacob, their unspoken pact resonating with determination, stepped into the heart of this mystical realm on their quest to hunt down malevolent witches.

As they ventured deeper, the woods whispered secrets long kept hidden. Shadows danced beneath the canopy, weaving tales of vengeful spirits and ancient curses. The air was thick with an otherworldly energy, and the trio felt the weight of the unseen eyes that watched their every move.

Their first target, a wicked witch rumored to have ensnared the forest in a web of dark magic, awaited justice. The enchanted scroll, a guide in their pursuit, unfurled cryptic symbols that illuminated their path. The cosmic dance between seekers and destiny continued, and the Whispering Woods became the stage for the next chapter of their supernatural odyssey.

Spectral apparitions materialized amid the ancient trees, their mournful whispers echoing through the woods. Gal, Jane, and Jacob, undeterred by the ethereal presence, pressed forward. The ancient magic that permeated the forest seemed to challenge their resolve, testing the very core of their purpose.

As they journeyed deeper into the woods, a mysterious figure emerged from the shadows. Cloaked in an ethereal glow, the figure revealed itself to be a guardian spirit—a keeper of the Whispering

Woods. With a voice that echoed through the ages, the spirit offered guidance to the seekers in their quest for justice.

"The wicked witch you seek has bound the spirits of this forest in chains of despair," the spirit intoned, its words carrying the weight of centuries. "To break her malevolent grip, you must navigate the realms of both the seen and the unseen. The cosmic forces have intertwined your destinies with the ancient spirits that call this forest home."

Gal, Jane, and Jacob absorbed the spirit's wisdom, realizing that their journey had become entwined with the very essence of the woods. The enchanted scroll, now resonating with a new energy, unveiled hidden passages and arcane symbols that would guide them through the labyrinthine depths of the Whispering Woods.

Their quest became a delicate dance between the tangible and the fantastical, the seen and the unseen. Shadows elongated and twisted beneath the ancient boughs as the trio followed the mystical guidance. The malevolent witch's presence grew palpable, a dark undercurrent that tainted the natural harmony of the forest.

The Whispering Woods, true to its name, seemed to communicate with the seekers through rustling leaves and creaking branches. The spirits, once shackled by the wicked witch's magic, whispered secrets of her hidden lair. The cosmic tapestry unfolded, revealing a convergence of destinies—a nexus of power where the witch drew strength from the captive spirits.

As they approached the heart of the woods, the spectral apparitions became more pronounced. Vengeful spirits, their ethereal forms twisted by the dark magic, emerged from the shadows. The malevolent witch, aware of the seekers' intrusion, unleashed illusions and phantoms to deter their progress.

Yet, guided by the spirit's wisdom and the enduring strength of their pact, Gal, Jane, and Jacob pressed on. The ancient trees bore witness to the cosmic dance between seekers and destiny, their leaves whispering encouragement as the trio faced the malevolent forces that sought to protect the witch's lair.

In the clearing at the heart of the Whispering Woods, the malevolent witch awaited—a sinister figure cloaked in shadows. The nexus of power, pulsating with dark energy, manifested before them. The quest for justice had reached its zenith, and the stage was set for a confrontation that would test the limits of the trio's courage.

With a shared glance of understanding, Gal, Jane, and Jacob readied themselves for the final reckoning. The Whispering Woods, with its secrets unveiled and spirits freed, bore witness to the cosmic forces that interwove the destinies of seekers and malevolent witches. The saga continued, echoing through the ancient trees, as the trio confronted the wicked witch in a battle that transcended the boundaries of the tangible and the fantastical.

The air in the heart of the Whispering Woods crackled with an otherworldly energy as Gal, Jane, and Jacob stepped into the clearing. The malevolent witch, shrouded in shadows, awaited them—a dark figure that seemed to draw power from the very essence of the enchanted realm.

The trio, guided by the spirit's wisdom and the revelations of the enchanted scroll, approached the nexus of power with caution. The ancient trees, their branches like outstretched arms, seemed to lend their silent support to the seekers' cause. The cosmic dance between seekers and destiny reached a crescendo, and the Whispering Woods became the backdrop for a battle that transcended the boundaries of reality.

The malevolent witch, sensing the intrusion, hissed with a voice that echoed through the ancient trees. "You dare challenge the forces that govern the unseen? Foolish mortals, you shall become mere shadows in my realm."

Undeterred, Gal, Jane, and Jacob stood firm. The enchanted scroll emanated a radiant glow, its symbols pulsating with a harmonious energy that seemed to counter the witch's malevolence. The spirits, now freed from their spectral shackles, whispered words of encouragement, their ethereal voices joining the cosmic chorus that enveloped the clearing.

The battle unfolded like a dance, a delicate interplay between the tangible and the fantastical. The malevolent witch unleashed dark magic, conjuring illusions that distorted the very fabric of reality. Phantoms emerged from the shadows, their ghostly forms a testament to the wickedness that had tainted the Whispering Woods.

Gal, empowered by the newfound knowledge gained from their previous encounters, wielded a talisman infused with the essence of the first amulet. Jane, armed with the strength of her friendship and the resolve forged through trials, brandished a mystical artifact gifted by the guardian spirit. Jacob, his experience as a survivor in the face of supernatural threats, gripped a silver dagger, its blade gleaming with an otherworldly light.

The nexus of power pulsated, responding to the clash between light and darkness. The Whispering Woods, once a realm ensnared by the malevolent witch's influence, now bore witness to a battle that sought to restore its natural harmony. The ancient trees seemed to sway in rhythm with the cosmic forces at play.

The malevolent witch, realizing the strength of the seekers' unity, intensified her onslaught. Dark tendrils of magic lashed out, attempting to ensnare the trio in an ethereal web. Illusions of fear and doubt manifested, threatening to unravel the bonds that held them together.

But the seekers, their spirits intertwined with the mystical forces that governed the Whispering Woods, stood resilient. With each stroke of the talisman, the mystical artifact, and the silver dagger, they chipped away at the witch's defenses. The spirits, now allies in the seekers' quest, lent their spectral energy to counter the malevolent forces.

As the battle reached its zenith, a blinding light erupted from the nexus of power. The malevolent witch, her dark form recoiling from the onslaught, let out a final, anguished scream. The Whispering Woods, bathed in the cleansing radiance, seemed to sigh with relief as the ancient magic that had bound it began to dissipate.

With a shared glance of understanding, Gal, Jane, and Jacob watched as the malevolent witch, weakened and defeated, faded into the shadows. The nexus of power, once a source of darkness, now pulsed with a serene light—a reflection of the restored harmony within the enchanted realm.

The Whispering Woods, liberated from the clutches of malevolence, stood silent. The ancient trees, witnesses to the cosmic dance between seekers and destiny, seemed to bow in acknowledgment. The saga of Gal, Jane, and Jacob had once again left its mark on the mystical unknown, echoing through the timeless tapestry of the enchanted forest.

As the seekers stepped out of the clearing, the Whispering Woods seemed to breathe with newfound life. The spirits, now free to roam, whispered words of gratitude. The enchanted scroll, its symbols fading, bore witness to the seekers' triumph, a testament to the enduring power of friendship in the face of cosmic forces.

And so, as the seekers ventured beyond the ancient trees, the Whispering Woods embraced its restored harmony. The cosmic dance continued, and the saga of Gal, Jane, and Jacob moved forward, leaving behind echoes of a battle that defied the boundaries of the tangible and the fantastical. The enchanted realm awaited its next chapter, and the seekers, undeterred, pressed on, ready to confront the unknown that lingered in the heart of the mystical tapestry.

The seekers ventured beyond the ancient trees, their footsteps resonating with a sense of accomplishment that reverberated through the Whispering Woods. The enchanted realm, now freed from the malevolent forces that once tainted its essence, seemed to breathe with renewed life. The cosmic dance continued, and the saga of Gal, Jane, and Jacob moved forward, leaving behind echoes of a battle that defied the boundaries of the tangible and the fantastical.

As they emerged from the Whispering Woods, the trio was greeted by the warm glow of the setting sun, casting long shadows on the forest floor. The air was filled with a tranquil serenity, a stark contrast to the intense struggle that had unfolded within the heart of the enchanted realm. The spirits, now liberated, lingered in the gentle breeze, their whispers fading into the harmonious symphony of nature.

Gal, Jane, and Jacob exchanged glances, their eyes reflecting the shared understanding of the profound journey they had undertaken. The enchanted forest, with its mysteries unveiled and malevolent entities vanquished, had become a chapter in their collective narrative—one that transcended the ordinary realms of existence.

A soft voice, carried by the wind, seemed to echo through the Whispering Woods. It was the guardian spirit, the mysterious figure that had guided them through the spectral apparitions and offered wisdom in the heart of the battle. "Seekers, your courage has restored the balance within this realm. The cosmic dance between seekers and destiny shall continue, and the echoes of your triumph will resonate through the ages."

With a nod of gratitude, Gal, Jane, and Jacob stepped out of the enchanted forest, their hearts lightened by the weight of the malevolent witch's defeat. The sun dipped below the horizon, casting hues of orange and pink across the sky, and the cosmic tapestry unfurled new threads that beckoned them forward.

The enchanted realm, now a testament to the seekers' resilience and the enduring power of friendship, faded into the background as the trio walked toward the horizon. The road stretched before them, a symbol of limitless possibilities, and the unknown awaited with its mysteries and challenges.

And so, as the seekers ventured into the dusk, the Whispering Woods embraced its restored harmony. The cosmic dance continued, and the saga of Gal, Jane, and Jacob moved forward, leaving behind echoes of a battle that defied the boundaries of the tangible and the fantastical. The enchanted realm, a part of their collective history, awaited its next chapter, ready to unfold in the ever-expanding tapestry of the mystical unknown.

The trio, undeterred by the cosmic forces that governed their destinies, pressed on with a shared sense of purpose and the enduring spirit that transcended the boundaries of the tangible and the fantastical. The Whispering Woods, now a beacon in the cosmic tapestry, watched them depart, its ancient trees standing as silent sentinels, guardians of the mystical realms that intertwined with the seekers' journey.

As the seekers disappeared into the fading light, the enchanted realm embraced the echoes of their triumph, a timeless testament to the enduring power of friendship against the forces that lurked in the mystical unknown. The saga continued, and the seekers, guided by the cosmic dance, moved forward into the night, ready to confront the unknown that lingered in the heart of the ever-unfolding tapestry.

Chapter 11: Coven's Conspiracy

The seekers, Gal, Jane, and Jacob, followed the cryptic trail of mystical symbols that wound through the tapestry of the cosmic unknown. Their journey led them to a small town nestled at the edge of the ordinary and the mystical—a place harboring a secret coven, where shadows whispered of dark rituals and sinister conspiracies.

As they entered the town, an unsettling hush hung in the air. The cobblestone streets seemed to echo with the footsteps of hidden entities, and the flickering street lamps cast long shadows that danced with an otherworldly rhythm. The seekers exchanged glances, a silent acknowledgment of the challenges that lay ahead in this enigmatic chapter of their journey.

The symbols guided them to an ancient-looking building obscured by overgrown vines—a facade that concealed the clandestine activities within. The trio hesitated before the entrance, the weight of the unknown pressing upon them. Gal, with her unyielding determination, took the lead, pushing the heavy wooden door ajar. They stepped into the dimly lit interior, where the air carried a palpable tension.

Inside, the seekers discovered a hidden chamber adorned with intricate symbols and adorned with flickering candles. Hooded figures, members of the secret coven, were engaged in an ominous ritual. The atmosphere crackled with mystic energy, and the air seemed to thicken with each uttered incantation.

As the trio observed from the shadows, they unraveled the plot—a conspiracy to summon a powerful entity that could tip the balance between the tangible and the fantastical. The coven, driven by desires that transcended the ordinary, sought to wield forces beyond mortal comprehension.

Gal, Jane, and Jacob exchanged whispers, formulating a plan to thwart the coven's dark ambitions. Their alliance, forged in the crucible of past challenges, faced a new test as the line between friend and foe blurred within the shadows of the clandestine chamber. The cosmic dance between seekers and destiny entered a new phase, where alliances would be tested, and the true nature of those they encountered would be unveiled.

With calculated precision, the seekers navigated the hidden corridors of the town, uncovering layers of the conspiracy that stretched beyond the secret coven. The dark rituals, intricately woven into the fabric of the town's history, hinted at a malevolent force that sought to breach the boundaries of reality.

Alliances formed and crumbled, trust wavered, and the seekers found themselves entangled in a web of deceit that threatened to ensnare them. Jacob's past, shrouded in mystery, became a focal point as the secrets of the town and the coven intertwined with his enigmatic existence.

As the seekers delved deeper into the mysteries, the small town revealed its darkest secrets—a history tainted by forbidden knowledge and a thirst for power. The cosmic forces, silent observers of the seekers' journey, seemed to intensify the challenges, testing the resilience of their friendship against the malevolent conspiracies that sought to manipulate the very fabric of reality.

The climax of the chapter unfolded in the heart of the coven's lair. The summoning ritual reached its zenith, and the seekers faced a choice that would define the outcome of the cosmic dance. The powerful entity, on the verge of manifestation, cast an ominous glow upon the chamber, and the seekers braced themselves for a confrontation that transcended the boundaries of the tangible and the fantastical.

In a surge of determination, Gal, Jane, and Jacob disrupted the ritual, breaking the intricate patterns that bound the entity to the mortal realm. The chamber erupted in chaos as mystic energies clashed, and the seekers fought against the coven's desperate attempts to salvage their plans.

As the last echoes of the disrupted ritual faded, the seekers emerged victorious but changed. The coven, dismantled and scattered, left behind a town liberated from the malevolent forces that had manipulated its destiny. The cosmic dance between seekers and destiny had weathered the storm, leaving the trio with newfound strength and a deeper understanding of the intricate threads that wove their intertwined destinies.

With the town restored to an uneasy calm, the seekers stepped into the night, their eyes reflecting the echoes of the conspiracies they had unraveled. The cosmic forces, silent spectators of this chapter, watched as Gal, Jane, and Jacob moved forward, leaving behind a town that bore witness to the resilience of friendship against the machinations of the mystical unknown.

The chapter concluded with a sense of accomplishment, but the lingering shadows hinted at more challenges awaiting the seekers. The cosmic dance continued, and the saga of Gal, Jane, and Jacob pressed on, leaving behind echoes of a conspiracy that had tested the limits of their alliance in the ever-unfolding tapestry of the unknown.

As the seekers stepped out of the town, the cool night air embraced them, carrying with it a mixture of relief and anticipation. The echoes of the coven's conspiracy lingered, creating a haunting melody that intertwined with the cosmic dance of the mystical unknown.

Gal, Jane, and Jacob shared a glance of understanding, acknowledging that the challenges they faced were mere threads in the intricate tapestry of their journey. The chapter of the coven's conspiracy had tested the limits of their alliance, revealing the strength forged through trials and the unyielding bond that held them together.

The cosmic forces, ever watchful, seemed to stir as the seekers moved forward, leaving the town behind. The night sky above them held secrets yet unrevealed, and the road stretched ahead—an endless path that promised more challenges, mysteries, and revelations.

With each step, the trio embraced the unknown, ready to confront the next chapter of their saga. The cosmic dance continued, a dance that defied the boundaries of the tangible and the fantastical. The lingering shadows cast by the coven's conspiracy hinted at a deeper cosmic design, one that tested the seekers' resilience and unveiled the enigmatic forces that guided their destinies.

As they ventured into the night, the road became a symbol of limitless possibilities. The seekers, undeterred by the shadows that clung to their past, pressed on with a shared sense of purpose. The cosmic dance had not reached its crescendo; it pulsed with the rhythm of the unknown, a rhythm that resonated through the seekers' hearts.

Gal, Jane, and Jacob rode the currents of the cosmic tapestry, their destinies entwined in a dance that spanned realms beyond mortal comprehension. The challenges they faced were but stepping stones, guiding them toward a greater understanding of the forces that lurked in the mystical corners of the universe.

The night unfolded, revealing a landscape shrouded in mystery. The seekers, guided by an unspoken pact and the echoes of their past victories, embraced the uncertainty. The saga of Gal, Jane, and Jacob continued—a relentless force in the cosmic dance between seekers and destiny.

And so, under the celestial canopy, the seekers pressed forward. The cosmic forces, ever shifting and enigmatic, awaited the unfolding of the next chapter. The echoes of the coven's conspiracy blended with the whispers of the night, creating a symphony that carried the seekers toward the heart of the mystical unknown.

The road stretched before them, winding through landscapes both ordinary and extraordinary. With each passing mile, the seekers left behind the shadows of the coven's conspiracy, stepping into the uncharted territories that awaited them. The cosmic dance, an eternal rhythm that guided their destinies, played on.

As the pickup truck carrying Gal, Jane, and Jacob disappeared into the vastness of the night, the cosmic forces continued their silent vigil. The saga of seekers and destiny, a tale woven with threads of friendship, mysticism, and resilience, etched its mark on the cosmic tapestry—an ever-unfolding narrative that defied the boundaries of the tangible and the fantastical.

And so, with the echoes of the coven's conspiracy behind them, the seekers ventured into the unknown, ready to confront the next enigma that awaited in the ever-unfolding tapestry of the mystical realms. The cosmic dance persisted, an eternal rhythm that guided the destinies of Gal, Jane, and Jacob, leaving behind echoes of a journey that transcended the ordinary and embraced the boundless possibilities of the cosmic unknown.

unknown. The road stretched ahead, a serpentine path leading the seekers into the heart of the mystical realms. The whispers of the night intertwined with the cosmic forces, creating an ethereal symphony that resonated through the very fabric of their existence.

As the pickup truck rolled through the night, Gal, Jane, and Jacob shared a moment of silent reflection. The chapter of the coven's conspiracy had tested their bonds and forged an unspoken pact—an alliance that would carry them through the veiled mysteries that awaited.

The cosmic dance, an intricate choreography of fate and destiny, guided their journey. The seekers, undeterred by the shadows of the past, embraced the uncertainty that lay ahead. Each mile traveled brought them closer to the next enigma, the next challenge that would shape their destinies.

Under the starlit sky, the seekers found themselves at the crossroads of the ordinary and the extraordinary. The cosmic forces, woven into the very fabric of the universe, whispered secrets that only the intrepid could comprehend. Gal, Jane, and Jacob, bound by friendship and a shared purpose, pressed forward with unwavering determination.

As the night unfolded its mysteries, the pickup truck became a vessel navigating the currents of the cosmic tapestry. The echoes of their laughter, the scars of past battles, and the enigmatic forces at play melded into a narrative that defied mortal understanding. The seekers were no longer mere mortals; they were participants in a cosmic drama, dancing on the edge of the unknown.

And so, as the horizon beckoned with promises of new adventures, the seekers embraced the boundless possibilities that the cosmic unknown presented. The road, a metaphor for the journey that transcended the ordinary, carried them into the heart of the mystical realms.

With a shared glance of understanding, Gal, Jane, and Jacob welcomed the next chapter. The cosmic dance continued, a timeless rhythm that echoed through the eons. The saga of seekers and destiny, etched into the very essence of the universe, unfolded with each passing moment.

As the pickup truck disappeared into the winding roads, the seekers became one with the cosmic forces. The echoes of the coven's conspiracy were but a distant melody, replaced by the anticipation of what lay beyond the horizon. The cosmic dance persisted, an eternal symphony playing out in the unseen realms.

And so, the seekers ventured into the heart of the unknown, carried by the cosmic currents that guided their destinies. The saga of Gal, Jane, and Jacob continued—a testament to the enduring spirit of friendship, the mysteries that lingered in the cosmic corners, and the boundless possibilities that awaited those willing to embrace the cosmic dance.

Chapter 12: Midnight Ritual

The moon hung low in the velvety sky, casting an ethereal glow over the landscape as the trio—Gal, Jane, and Jacob—approached the clandestine ritual site. The air crackled with an otherworldly energy, a palpable tension that hinted at the forbidden ceremony unfolding in the hidden depths of the night.

The seekers, armed with knowledge gleaned from their previous encounters, moved silently through the shadows. The Whispering Woods had prepared them for the unknown, and the lessons learned in the haunted realms resonated within their beings. The cosmic dance, an ever-present force guiding their destinies, propelled them toward the heart of the mystical confrontation.

As they neared the ritual site, the faint hum of incantations reached their ears. Mystical symbols adorned the perimeter, marking the boundary between the mundane and the supernatural. Gal, Jane, and Jacob exchanged a glance, a silent affirmation of their shared purpose—the unraveling of the malevolent forces orchestrating the midnight ritual.

The clearing came into view, bathed in an eerie luminescence. A circle of cloaked figures, the coven, stood in solemn reverence. Candles flickered, casting dancing shadows that seemed to merge with the cosmic forces at play. In the center of the circle, an ancient tome lay open, its pages whispering secrets to those who dared to listen.

Gal tightened her grip on the enchanted dagger, a relic from their previous battles. Jane clutched a vial containing sacred water, and Jacob wielded a staff adorned with symbols that resonated with ancient power. The seekers, their resolve unyielding, prepared to disrupt the malevolent dance that threatened to tip the cosmic balance.

The first clash of spells echoed through the midnight air as the seekers revealed themselves. The coven, startled but undeterred, turned their attention toward the intruders. The cosmic dance reached a crescendo, a symphony of arcane energies colliding in a spectacle that transcended mortal understanding.

Gal, with a swift motion, traced protective symbols in the air, creating a barrier that deflected the malevolent spells. Jane, attuned to the elemental forces, unleashed torrents of sacred water, disrupting the coven's carefully orchestrated ritual. Jacob chanted incantations, invoking the ancient spirits to aid their cause.

The midnight ritual became a battleground, a clash of mystical forces that reverberated through the unseen realms. Shadows danced in a chaotic display, merging with the cosmic tapestry that hung suspended in the midnight air. The outcome of the confrontation hung in the balance, a delicate equilibrium that teetered on the edge of cosmic chaos.

As the seekers fought against the malevolent witches, the ancient tome emitted a pulsating glow. The pages turned on their own accord, revealing forgotten incantations and forbidden knowledge. The cosmic dance responded to the unfolding drama, weaving the destinies of the seekers with the threads of the mystical unknown.

A surge of power emanated from the center of the ritual site, enveloping the seekers in an arcane embrace. Gal, Jane, and Jacob felt the cosmic forces coursing through their veins, amplifying their abilities. The seekers, momentarily infused with otherworldly energy, pressed forward with renewed determination.

The clash intensified, a maelstrom of spells and counter-spells that defied mortal comprehension. The seekers, guided by the cosmic dance, unleashed their own potent incantations, pushing back against the malevolent forces. The midnight air became charged with the scent of magic, a heady mixture of power and ancient knowledge.

In the midst of the cosmic turmoil, a figure emerged from the shadows—the leader of the coven, a formidable witch whose eyes glowed with an unnatural fervor. The seekers, undeterred by the imposing presence, focused their efforts on disrupting the ritual at its core.

As Gal traced intricate patterns in the air, Jane summoned gusts of wind that swirled around the ancient tome. Jacob, tapping into the ley lines that crisscrossed the ritual site, directed the cosmic energies toward the epicenter of the midnight dance. The seekers, in unison, chanted a counter-incantation, a fusion of their unique abilities.

The cosmic dance responded, acknowledging the seekers' resilience in the face of malevolent forces. The ritual site quivered, the very fabric of the mystical unknown unraveling in response to the seekers' disruption. The coven, realizing the precariousness of their endeavor, intensified their efforts in a desperate bid to salvage the midnight ritual.

In a final surge of cosmic energy, the seekers' incantation reached its zenith. The ancient tome, unable to withstand the opposing forces, disintegrated into a burst of ethereal sparks. The coven, their source of power shattered, recoiled in shock as the cosmic dance tilted in favor of the seekers.

The midnight air, once charged with arcane energies, began to settle. The mystical symbols that adorned the ritual site dimmed, their glow fading into the shadows. The cosmic forces, having witnessed the seekers' triumph, echoed their victory in the unseen realms.

The leader of the coven, her powers weakened, retreated into the shadows. The remaining cloaked figures dispersed, their malevolent intentions thwarted by the seekers' resilience. Gal, Jane, and Jacob, standing amidst the remnants of the midnight ritual, exchanged glances of exhaustion and triumph.

The cosmic dance, having played witness to the seekers' valor, continued its eternal rhythm. The midnight ritual, a chapter in their ongoing saga, had tested the limits of their abilities and forged a deeper connection with the cosmic forces that guided their destinies.

As the echoes of the confrontation lingered in the midnight air, the seekers acknowledged the ever-unfolding tapestry of the mystical unknown. The cosmic dance persisted, an intricate choreography that entwined the destinies of Gal, Jane, and Jacob with the unseen forces that watched their journey unfold.

And so, as the seekers stood in the aftermath of the midnight ritual, the cosmic dance beckoned them toward the next chapter. The road stretched ahead, a serpentine path leading into the heart of the mystical realms. The saga of Gal, Jane, and Jacob continued, leaving behind echoes of a battle that defied the boundaries of the tangible and the fantastical.

As they ventured into the unknown, the seekers embraced the enduring spirit of friendship and the mysteries that awaited in the cosmic corners. The midnight ritual, a testament to their resilience, faded into the cosmic tapestry—a tale whispered through the cosmic winds, echoing the eternal dance between seekers and destiny.

And so, with the remnants of the midnight ritual dissipating into the cosmic tapestry, the seekers—Gal, Jane, and Jacob—embarked on the next phase of their journey into the unknown. The echoes of their triumph resonated through the unseen realms, a testament to the enduring spirit of friendship that bound them together in the face of mystical challenges.

The Whispering Woods, the Island of the Undead, the Cornfield of Nightmares—all were chapters in their saga, each leaving an indelible mark on the seekers' understanding of the mystical unknown. The cosmic dance continued, an eternal rhythm that guided their destinies and beckoned them toward new horizons.

As the seekers traversed the winding paths of the enchanted realm, their senses attuned to the subtle energies that lingered in the air, they found themselves drawn to an ancient gateway—a portal that shimmered with an otherworldly luminescence. The cosmic forces, ever-present and enigmatic, whispered secrets of another dimension awaiting exploration.

Gal, Jane, and Jacob exchanged glances filled with anticipation, their shared understanding unspoken yet profound. The portal, a threshold to realms yet undiscovered, invited them to step into the cosmic dance with hearts open to the mysteries that awaited. The seekers, hand in hand, approached the threshold, ready to confront the next enigma woven into the fabric of the mystical tapestry.

The transition through the portal was a kaleidoscope of cosmic energies, swirling hues that transcended mortal comprehension. As the seekers emerged on the other side, they found themselves in a realm unlike any they had encountered before—an ethereal landscape where the boundaries of reality and fantasy converged.

The Whispering Winds, gentle breezes carrying whispers of ancient knowledge, guided them deeper into this uncharted dimension. The seekers walked through landscapes painted with hues that defied earthly descriptions, encountering beings of light and shadow that acknowledged their presence with cryptic nods.

With every step, the seekers felt the pulse of the cosmic dance resonating beneath their feet. The echoes of their past encounters merged with the unseen melodies of this new realm, creating a symphony that told tales of forgotten civilizations and untold mysteries waiting to be unraveled.

As the seekers delved further into the heart of the dimension, they stumbled upon an ancient library—an archive of cosmic wisdom guarded by ethereal scribes. The books, bound in luminescent materials, beckoned them with promises of insights into the very nature of the cosmic dance.

Gal, Jane, and Jacob, their curiosity aflame, immersed themselves in the tomes that lined the celestial shelves. Each page revealed fragments of cosmic truths, unraveling the secrets of the interconnected realms and the mystical forces that governed their destinies.

In the quiet recesses of the celestial library, the seekers discovered a mural—an intricate tapestry that depicted their journey from the first whispers of the cosmic winds to the triumph over the midnight ritual. The mural extended, unveiling chapters yet to be written, cosmic threads waiting to be woven into the ongoing dance.

With newfound knowledge and a deeper connection to the cosmic forces, the seekers continued their exploration of the uncharted dimension. The portal, a cosmic doorway between realms, awaited their return, signaling the ever-unfolding tapestry that bound them to the mystical unknown.

As the seekers stepped back through the portal, the luminescence of the celestial library faded behind them. The Whispering Winds guided their journey, and the cosmic dance embraced them with an eternal rhythm—a dance that defied the boundaries of time and space.

And so, under the ordinary sky, amidst the familiar streets, the trio stepped into the next chapter of their lives—a testament to the resilience of friendship, the mysteries that lingered in the cosmic corners, and the enduring spirit that transcended the boundaries of the tangible and the fantastical.

The saga of Gal, Jane, and Jacob continued, leaving an indelible mark on the unseen realms that watched their journey unfold. The road stretched before them, a symbol of limitless possibilities, as they embraced the unknown with a shared sense of purpose and the enduring power of friendship.

As the seekers ventured into the next chapter, the cosmic dance persisted—an eternal rhythm that guided their destinies through the ever-unfolding tapestry of the mystical realms. The echoes of their laughter, the whispers of mystical encounters, and the shared glances of understanding resonated through the cosmic winds, echoing a tale that defied the boundaries of the tangible and the fantastical.

And so, the seekers pressed on, ready for new adventures, cosmic forces guiding their way. The unseen realms awaited the continuation of their saga, a dance that transcended the ordinary and embraced the boundless possibilities of the cosmic.

As the seekers pressed on, their journey through the cosmic unknown took them to realms that defied mortal imagination. The Whispering Winds guided them to landscapes bathed in celestial hues, where celestial beings whispered secrets of forgotten realms.

Each step was a testament to the enduring spirit of friendship, the cosmic dance guiding their destinies through realms uncharted. Gal, Jane, and Jacob, hand in hand, traversed through dimensions where time flowed like a river of stardust, and the boundaries between reality and fantasy blurred into a cosmic dreamscape.

The seekers encountered celestial creatures—guardians of the cosmic tapestry—who acknowledged their presence with ethereal nods. The murmurs of the unseen realms intertwined with the seekers' footsteps, creating a symphony that echoed through the cosmic corridors.

In the heart of this cosmic expanse, the seekers discovered a celestial observatory—a place where constellations whispered tales of ancient civilizations and cosmic wonders. The seekers gazed upon celestial maps, unraveling the interconnected threads that bound their destinies to the vastness of the cosmos.

The whispers of the stars spoke of a cosmic convergence, a moment where seekers and destiny would dance in harmony. The seekers, attuned to the cosmic rhythms, felt the pulse of a celestial phenomenon approaching—a revelation that awaited at the cosmic crossroads.

Underneath the celestial canopy, the seekers found themselves at the Cosmic Crossroads—a nexus where past, present, and future coalesced into a cosmic tableau. Here, the cosmic forces revealed fragments of their next chapter, cosmic threads waiting to be woven into the ever-unfolding tapestry.

Gal, Jane, and Jacob, their eyes reflecting the constellations' luminescence, stood at the threshold of cosmic revelations. The unseen realms held secrets that beckoned to be explored, challenges that called for their resilience, and mysteries that yearned to be unraveled.

The Whispering Winds, a gentle breeze carrying the cosmic chorus, encouraged the seekers to embrace the boundless possibilities of the cosmic. As they ventured forward, the cosmic dance persisted—an eternal rhythm that guided their destinies through the infinite realms.

And so, with a shared glance of understanding, the seekers stepped into the cosmic dance once more. The echoes of their laughter, the whispers of mystical encounters, and the shared glances of understanding resonated through the cosmic winds, leaving behind traces of a journey that transcended the ordinary.

The seekers, undeterred by the mysteries that awaited, embraced the cosmic dance with open hearts. The cosmic tapestry, a canvas painted with the hues of their adventures, awaited the strokes of the seekers as they moved forward into the boundless possibilities that awaited.

As the seekers vanished into the cosmic horizon, their laughter echoed through the celestial corridors, leaving an indelible mark on the unseen realms. The cosmic dance continued, an eternal rhythm that guided the destinies of Gal, Jane, and Jacob—a testament to the enduring power of friendship in the cosmic ballet.

And so, the saga of the seekers unfolded, leaving behind whispers of a journey that embraced the cosmic unknown. The unseen realms, illuminated by the seekers' cosmic footsteps, awaited the continuation of their dance—a dance that transcended the ordinary and embraced the boundless possibilities of the cosmic.

Chapter 13: The Seer's Warning

In the cosmic expanse where the seekers tread, the celestial winds whispered of an imminent encounter with a seer—an ancient oracle whose eyes held the reflections of eons past and future. The seekers, Gal, Jane, and Jacob, found themselves drawn to the enigmatic presence of the Seer's Warning—a chapter that would shape the trajectory of their cosmic journey.

As they ventured deeper into the cosmic unknown, the ambient glow of ethereal constellations guided them to a place where shadows seemed to dance in rhythm with the cosmic heartbeat. The Seer's presence manifested, her figure emerging from the interplay of shadows and starlight.

The Seer, draped in robes adorned with celestial patterns, stood before the seekers with eyes ablaze—an ancient wisdom reflected in the depths of her gaze. The cosmic tapestry whispered tales of her prescience, a seer who navigated the currents of time and space with unparalleled insight.

"Seekers," the Seer's voice resonated through the cosmic winds, "you have woven threads in the tapestry of fate, threads that now attract the attention of forces beyond your reckoning."

Gal, Jane, and Jacob exchanged glances, sensing the gravity of the cosmic revelations that awaited them. The Seer extended her hand, and a celestial projection unfolded—a vision of an otherworldly adversary, a cosmic force seeking revenge for the seekers' meddling in the affairs of witches.

"The cosmic balance is delicate, and your actions have set in motion a cosmic tempest," the Seer intoned. "A force awakens—a primordial entity that seeks retribution for the disturbance caused by meddling mortals. You face a choice, seekers: abandon your quest and fade into the cosmic background, or confront an adversary beyond your comprehension."

The seekers, their faces illuminated by the celestial glow, contemplated the weight of the Seer's words. Abandoning their quest meant relinquishing the cosmic dance, the boundless possibilities that beckoned them. Confronting an otherworldly adversary meant embracing a challenge that transcended mortal understanding.

Gal, ever resilient, spoke with determination, "We cannot turn away from the cosmic journey we've embarked upon. We choose to confront this cosmic force, whatever it may be."

The Seer nodded, her eyes reflecting approval mingled with a hint of sorrow. "Very well, seekers. The path you tread will lead you to the cosmic battleground—a realm where mortal courage will be tested against the cosmic unknown."

With a wave of her hand, the Seer enveloped the seekers in a cosmic embrace. The celestial winds carried them through the cosmic currents, transporting them to the threshold of the impending confrontation. The cosmic tapestry unfolded, revealing glimpses of the cosmic force that awaited—an entity born from the fabric of the universe itself.

The seekers found themselves in a surreal realm, where reality shimmered like stardust and the echoes of cosmic battles reverberated through the astral plains. The cosmic force, a nebulous presence that defied mortal comprehension, loomed before them.

The Seer's warning echoed in their minds as the cosmic force stirred—an amalgamation of celestial energies coalescing into a cosmic tempest. Gal, Jane, and Jacob, standing at the epicenter of the cosmic battleground, braced themselves for a confrontation that would redefine the very essence of their existence.

The cosmic dance persisted, the seekers and the cosmic force entwined in a celestial ballet. Spells clashed, celestial energies collided, and the boundaries between mortal and cosmic forces blurred. The seekers, guided by the enduring spirit of friendship, faced the cosmic tempest with unwavering determination.

As the cosmic battle unfolded, the Seer's warning resonated in the seekers' hearts—an acknowledgment of the cosmic forces that sought equilibrium. The battleground became a canvas for the cosmic dance, where mortal courage clashed with celestial might.

And so, under the astral canopy, the seekers pressed forward, embracing the cosmic dance with open hearts. The Seer's warning lingered in the cosmic winds, a reminder of the delicate balance that governed the realms beyond mortal perception.

The echoes of the cosmic battle faded into the celestial expanse, leaving behind traces of a chapter that tested the limits of mortal courage. The seekers, undeterred by the cosmic forces that sought revenge, continued their journey through the boundless possibilities of the cosmic unknown.

The Seer, her figure disappearing into the cosmic currents, whispered words of encouragement that lingered in the seekers' hearts. The cosmic tapestry awaited further threads, and the saga of Gal, Jane, and Jacob continued—a testament to the enduring spirit of friendship in the cosmic dance between seekers and destiny.

As the seekers ventured deeper into the cosmic unknown, the celestial winds carried whispers of new chapters waiting to be written. The Seer's warning, a beacon in the astral tapestry, guided them forward, leaving behind echoes of a journey that transcended mortal boundaries and embraced the cosmic possibilities that awaited in the heart of the mystical realms.

The seekers, Gal, Jane, and Jacob, navigated the cosmic currents with a renewed sense of purpose, guided by the ethereal echoes of the Seer's warning. The astral winds whispered of new chapters unfurling in the cosmic tapestry, and the trio pressed forward into the heart of the mystical realms—a realm where the boundaries between the tangible and the fantastical melted away.

The cosmic currents carried them to an enchanting realm, where luminescent landscapes unfolded like pages in a cosmic tome. Celestial flora swayed to the rhythm of unseen forces, and constellations painted the astral sky with hues unseen by mortal eyes. As the seekers traversed this ethereal landscape, the whispers of cosmic possibilities surrounded them.

Gal, her gaze fixed on the celestial horizon, felt the cosmic energies resonating within her. The journey had become more than a quest against malevolent witches; it had transformed into a cosmic odyssey, an exploration of the mystical unknown that lay beyond the veil of mortal perception.

Jane, her senses attuned to the astral melodies, marveled at the beauty that transcended earthly understanding. "This is beyond anything we could have imagined," she whispered, her voice carried by the cosmic winds.

Jacob, ever vigilant, scanned the astral surroundings, sensing the ebb and flow of celestial energies. "The Seer's warning guided us here for a reason," he remarked. "There's a cosmic purpose waiting to be unveiled."

As the seekers journeyed through the astral landscapes, they stumbled upon an ancient observatory—a structure that bridged the realms of mortal and cosmic knowledge. Intricate patterns adorned the observatory's celestial dome, depicting constellations that mirrored the seekers' past and hinted at the cosmic challenges yet to come.

Within the observatory, a celestial figure awaited—a cosmic guardian, a custodian of astral knowledge. The figure, cloaked in stardust, greeted the seekers with eyes that sparkled like distant galaxies.

"Seekers of the cosmic dance," the celestial figure intoned, "you stand at the crossroads of destinies, where mortal threads intertwine with celestial forces. The chapters written by your actions have caught the attention of the cosmic realms, and a cosmic purpose awaits your embrace."

Gal, Jane, and Jacob exchanged glances, their anticipation heightened by the celestial figure's words. The guardian extended a hand, and a cosmic projection unfolded—an astral map that revealed the next chapter in their cosmic journey.

"You are destined to traverse the Luminous Nexus—a realm where echoes of ancient wisdom resonate," the guardian explained. "There, you will face trials that challenge the very essence of your cosmic bonds. Embrace the unknown, seekers, for the Luminous Nexus awaits your cosmic dance."

With the celestial map in hand, the seekers exited the observatory, guided by the astral winds toward the Luminous Nexus. The cosmic currents carried them through astral gateways, realms of color and sound that transcended mortal comprehension.

As they entered the Luminous Nexus, the seekers felt a surge of cosmic energy enveloping them. Luminescent pathways materialized, leading them through an ethereal labyrinth where ancient voices whispered secrets of the cosmos.

The trials within the Luminous Nexus tested the seekers' understanding of cosmic forces. Celestial puzzles, astral riddles, and trials of courage awaited them at every turn. Yet, with each challenge faced, the seekers discovered new facets of their cosmic potential.

The echoes of their laughter resonated through the astral corridors, a testament to the enduring spirit of friendship that fueled their cosmic odyssey. The Luminous Nexus, with its radiant mysteries and cosmic revelations, became a crucible where mortal and celestial energies intertwined.

As the seekers reached the heart of the Luminous Nexus, a cosmic entity manifested—a being of pure astral energy, its form shifting like the dance of stardust. The entity spoke with a voice that echoed across galaxies.

"Seekers, your journey has not gone unnoticed in the cosmic tapestry," the astral entity proclaimed. "The Luminous Nexus has revealed the strength of your cosmic bonds, and you are now entrusted with a cosmic purpose greater than you can fathom."

The seekers, humbled by the cosmic revelations, nodded in acknowledgment. The astral entity bestowed upon them celestial artifacts—manifestations of cosmic potential that would aid them in the challenges that lay ahead.

"And so," the entity concluded, "embrace your cosmic purpose. The Luminous Nexus was but a prelude to the chapters yet to be written in the cosmic tapestry. Seekers, continue your dance between mortal and celestial forces, for the cosmic realms await your next steps."

With a celestial blessing, the seekers emerged from the Luminous Nexus, their cosmic artifacts shimmering with astral radiance. The astral winds carried them forward, and the whispers of new chapters filled the cosmic tapestry.

As the seekers ventured into the unknown, the cosmic dance persisted—a timeless rhythm that guided them through the mystical realms. The saga of Gal, Jane, and Jacob continued, leaving behind echoes of their journey imprinted on the celestial fabric that wove through the boundless possibilities of the cosmic unknown.

In the wake of their journey through the Luminous Nexus, the seekers—Gal, Jane, and Jacob—emerged into an astral expanse that transcended the limits of mortal understanding. The celestial energies resonated with echoes of ancient wisdom, and the trio carried the luminous artifacts bestowed upon them by the astral entity.

The astral winds guided them to the edge of the cosmic unknown, where an ethereal gateway shimmered like a veil between dimensions.

As they approached, the celestial fabric pulsed with the cosmic rhythms, welcoming the seekers to the next chapter of their odyssey.

With shared glances of understanding, the trio stepped through the astral gateway, the cosmic dance persisting as they traversed the boundary between the familiar and the undiscovered. The astral currents carried them into a realm where time flowed like a river of stardust, and constellations formed patterns that whispered tales of forgotten epochs.

In this cosmic expanse, the seekers encountered celestial beings—guardians of astral realms, each embodying the essence of cosmic forces. The beings bestowed upon them cryptic prophecies and insights into the celestial dance that shaped destinies across the cosmos.

As the seekers delved deeper into the astral realms, they stumbled upon a cosmic nexus—a convergence point where threads of fate intertwined. The nexus revealed glimpses of parallel dimensions, alternate realities, and cosmic events that reverberated through the cosmic tapestry.

The whispers of the cosmic winds guided the seekers to a cosmic library—a repository of cosmic knowledge guarded by ethereal scribes. The scribes, their forms ever-shifting like celestial constellations, shared tales of cosmic battles, mystical artifacts, and the interplay between mortal and cosmic forces.

In their quest for understanding, the seekers uncovered the existence of an ancient prophecy—a cosmic rhyme that echoed through the astral realms. The prophecy hinted at a convergence of cosmic energies, a celestial alignment that would test the seekers' mettle and reshape the destinies of worlds.

The celestial artifacts glowed with newfound vigor, resonating with the cosmic energies that surrounded them. Gal, Jane, and Jacob realized that their journey had become intricately entwined with the cosmic forces steering the course of existence.

With a shared resolve, the seekers embraced the cosmic prophecy, knowing that the threads of destiny were intertwined with their choices. The astral currents guided them toward the epicenter of the cosmic convergence, where celestial energies pulsed with the intensity of a cosmic heartbeat.

As they reached the nexus of cosmic forces, the seekers witnessed the cosmic alignment—a celestial dance that transcended the boundaries of time and space. The cosmic energies surged, and the seekers felt an otherworldly power coursing through their beings.

A luminous figure materialized before them—the embodiment of the cosmic convergence. With eyes ablaze with astral fire, the figure spoke in a voice that echoed through the astral realms.

"Seekers of the cosmic dance," the figure intoned, "you have embraced the threads of destiny and navigated the cosmic tapestry with unwavering purpose. The convergence has unveiled your cosmic potential, and the choices you make will resonate through the fabric of existence."

Gal, Jane, and Jacob, humbled by the cosmic revelations, gazed at the celestial figure with a mixture of awe and determination. The cosmic energies surged around them, and the luminous artifacts responded with radiant brilliance.

"As you continue your cosmic journey," the figure continued, "remember that every step shapes the cosmic dance. Embrace the boundless possibilities that await, for your saga has become an indelible thread in the tapestry of the cosmic unknown."

With a cosmic blessing, the figure dissipated into astral light, and the seekers found themselves back at the edge of the astral gateway. The celestial artifacts glowed with the residual energies of the cosmic convergence, and the astral winds beckoned them to step through the gateway once more.

As they crossed the threshold between the cosmic realms, the astral currents guided the seekers back to the familiar realm—the realm where their journey had begun. The echoes of the cosmic convergence lingered, and the seekers knew that their saga had entered a new phase, marked by the cosmic dance that intertwined the destinies of Gal, Jane, and Jacob.

With a shared understanding, the trio stepped back into the ordinary world, their cosmic artifacts pulsating with astral radiance. The cosmic dance persisted, leaving behind echoes of a journey that defied mortal boundaries and embraced the boundless possibilities of the cosmic unknown.

And so, under the ordinary sky, amidst the familiar streets, the saga of Gal, Jane, and Jacob continued—an indomitable force in the cosmic dance between seekers and destiny. The road stretched before them, a symbol of limitless possibilities, as they embraced the unknown with a shared sense of purpose and the enduring power of friendship. The cosmic dance persisted, an eternal rhythm guiding them through the mystical realms, leaving behind echoes of a journey imprinted on the celestial fabric that wove through the boundless possibilities of the cosmic unknown.

Chapter 14: Celestial Confrontation

In the wake of the cosmic convergence, Gal, Jane, and Jacob found themselves standing on the precipice of a desolate realm where cosmic energies intertwined like threads in a celestial tapestry. The astral winds whispered secrets of a vengeful force seeking retribution—an entity born from the misuse of witchcraft across dimensions.

The trio braced themselves as the cosmic currents guided them deeper into the cosmic unknown. The celestial landscape shifted, revealing a realm where stars flickered with ethereal brilliance, and the very fabric of reality seemed to quiver with cosmic potential.

As they ventured forth, the seekers encountered the celestial force—a manifestation of cosmic wrath with eyes that gleamed with the collective anger of misused mystical energies. The vengeful entity spoke in resonant echoes that reverberated through the astral expanse.

"Seekers of the cosmic dance," the entity intoned, "you tread upon the realms where mortal actions intertwine with cosmic consequences. The threads of misuse have birthed me, a force seeking balance in the cosmic tapestry."

Gal, Jane, and Jacob exchanged determined glances, ready to confront the vengeful force and resolve the cosmic imbalance wrought by the misuse of witchcraft. The celestial battlefield unfolded before them—a cosmic arena where stars became ethereal witnesses to the impending confrontation.

The vengeful entity unleashed cosmic energies, manifesting ethereal tendrils that reached across dimensions. The seekers felt the weight of their cosmic potential, their astral artifacts pulsating with the energies of the recent convergence. The celestial battle began, an intricate dance between mortals and cosmic forces.

Gal, empowered by the cosmic energies, exhibited newfound abilities—a fusion of mortal resilience and astral prowess. She conjured ethereal shields, deflecting the cosmic onslaught unleashed by the vengeful force. Jane harnessed the celestial winds, weaving them into intricate spells that disrupted the entity's ethereal tendrils.

Jacob, his connection to the cosmic forces deepened by his previous encounters, summoned ethereal allies—manifestations of astral beings that joined the seekers in their celestial struggle. The cosmic battlefield echoed with the clash of ethereal forces, a dance of cosmic energies that transcended mortal understanding.

As the celestial confrontation unfolded, the seekers realized that the vengeful force drew its strength from the cosmic imbalances caused by malevolent witches across dimensions. Each ethereal tendril mirrored the actions of those who had misused mystical powers, creating a cosmic resonance that threatened to unravel the very fabric of reality.

Gal, Jane, and Jacob, undeterred by the cosmic chaos, pressed forward. They channeled their collective energy, forming an astral bond that resonated with the cosmic threads of destiny. The vengeful force, sensing the unity of mortals and cosmic potential, intensified its cosmic onslaught.

The seekers delved into the depths of the cosmic unknown, where ethereal patterns revealed the origins of the vengeful force. They discovered that the entity was an amalgamation of cosmic energies tainted by the malevolent actions of witches in various dimensions. The cosmic resonance echoed the struggles of the seekers' past encounters, intertwining their destinies with the larger cosmic narrative.

With newfound knowledge, the seekers aimed to sever the ethereal tendrils and cleanse the cosmic energies tainted by the misuse of witchcraft. Gal, Jane, and Jacob synchronized their abilities, weaving a celestial symphony that resonated through the astral expanse.

As the seekers reached the epicenter of the celestial battlefield, they encountered the core of the vengeful force—a swirling vortex of cosmic energies entwined with malevolent intentions. The seekers channeled their astral artifacts, focusing their energy to disrupt the cosmic resonance and restore balance to the realms.

The celestial confrontation reached its zenith—a crescendo of ethereal energies clashing and intertwining. The vengeful force, now confronted by the seekers' unity and resolve, began to dissipate. The astral winds carried echoes of cosmic rebalancing, as the threads of destiny realigned with a harmonious cosmic dance.

In the aftermath of the celestial confrontation, the cosmic energies subsided, and the astral landscape regained its serenity. Gal, Jane, and Jacob stood amidst the celestial aftermath, their astral artifacts glowing with a gentle radiance.

The vengeful force, once a manifestation of cosmic imbalance, faded into the cosmic currents—a testament to the seekers' ability to navigate the intricate dance between mortals and celestial forces. The threads of destiny, now untangled from the cosmic chaos, seemed to shimmer with newfound clarity.

As the seekers gazed upon the celestial expanse, the astral winds whispered tales of cosmic renewal. The realms, once marred by the misuse of witchcraft, now resonated with harmonious energies. The cosmic dance continued, and the seekers realized that their journey had become a pivotal chapter in the cosmic narrative.

With a shared sense of accomplishment, Gal, Jane, and Jacob stepped away from the celestial battlefield. The echoes of the celestial confrontation lingered, leaving behind a celestial imprint on the astral fabric that wove through the cosmic unknown.

And so, under the cosmic sky, amidst the celestial echoes, the saga of Gal, Jane, and Jacob continued—a cosmic force in the ever-unfolding dance between seekers and destiny. The road stretched before them, a cosmic tapestry woven with boundless possibilities, as they embraced the unknown with a shared purpose and the enduring power of friendship. The cosmic dance persisted, an eternal rhythm guiding them through the mystical realms, leaving behind echoes of a journey imprinted on the celestial fabric that wove through the boundless possibilities of the cosmic unknown.

As the seekers ventured into the cosmic unknown, the celestial winds carried whispers of new chapters waiting to be written. The road stretched before them, a cosmic tapestry woven with boundless possibilities, and the trio embraced the allure of the unknown with a shared purpose and the enduring power of friendship.

The astral echoes of their recent triumph reverberated through the cosmic expanse, leaving behind a trail of stardust that shimmered with the remnants of celestial energies. The cosmic dance persisted—an eternal rhythm that guided them through the mystical realms, and the seekers felt the pull of destiny intertwining with the cosmic threads.

Gal, Jane, and Jacob, undeterred by the cosmic challenges that lay ahead, continued their journey. Their astral artifacts, now attuned to the harmonious energies of the celestial aftermath, pulsed with a radiant glow. The cosmic unknown beckoned, and the seekers pressed forward, ready to confront the next enigma that awaited in the ever-unfolding tapestry of the mystical realms.

As they traversed the cosmic landscape, the seekers encountered astral gateways leading to realms untouched by mortal eyes. Ethereal forests whispered secrets, celestial oceans held reflections of distant galaxies, and astral mountains stood as silent sentinels in the cosmic vastness. Each step resonated with the echoes of their previous encounters, a testament to the cosmic journey that had reshaped their destinies.

The astral winds whispered tales of ancient prophecies, cosmic guardians, and realms where time danced to celestial melodies. The seekers, fueled by the shared purpose of their pact, delved into the mysteries that lingered in the heart of the cosmic unknown. The celestial forces guided their way, offering glimpses of the next chapter waiting to be unveiled.

In the cosmic tapestry, the seekers discovered a nexus of interconnected realms—a celestial hub where the boundaries between dimensions blurred. Here, cosmic energies pulsed with a vibrant intensity, creating a kaleidoscope of astral hues that painted the unseen realms in ethereal brilliance.

As they traversed the cosmic nexus, the seekers encountered celestial entities—guardians of the interdimensional pathways. These cosmic beings, adorned with starlight and astral energy, bestowed upon the trio ancient knowledge and astral artifacts infused with the essence of cosmic wisdom.

With each encounter, the seekers' understanding of the cosmic dance deepened. They learned to harness astral energies, commune with celestial spirits, and navigate the intricate pathways that connected the realms. The cosmic nexus, a convergence of destinies, became a pivotal chapter in their cosmic journey.

The seekers, now attuned to the celestial energies that resonated within them, stood at the threshold of a new astral realm. The cosmic dance persisted, and the tapestry of possibilities unfolded before them. The road stretched beyond the cosmic horizon, leading to realms where the boundaries of the tangible and the fantastical blended into a seamless dance of cosmic forces.

With a shared glance of understanding, the trio stepped into the astral realm, where echoes of ancient prophecies whispered through the cosmic winds. The celestial beings watched with benevolent eyes as the seekers embraced the unknown, their journey leaving an indelible mark on the cosmic fabric that wove through the boundless possibilities of the astral expanse.

And so, amidst the cosmic echoes, the saga of Gal, Jane, and Jacob continued—a cosmic force in the ever-unfolding dance between seekers and destiny. The road stretched before them, a cosmic tapestry woven with boundless possibilities, and the seekers, guided by the enduring power of friendship, ventured deeper into the mystical realms. The cosmic dance persisted—an eternal rhythm that resonated through the unseen corners of the astral expanse, leaving behind echoes of a journey that transcended the ordinary and embraced the limitless possibilities of the cosmic unknown.

As the seekers ventured deeper into the astral expanse, the cosmic dance persisted, echoing through the unseen corners of the mystical realms. The celestial entities, guardians of the cosmic tapestry, watched with benevolent eyes as the trio navigated the ethereal landscapes that unfolded before them.

In the cosmic tapestry, threads of destiny intertwined, weaving a narrative that surpassed mortal understanding. The seekers, fueled by the enduring spirit of friendship and the cosmic forces that guided them, pressed on toward realms where the boundaries of reality and fantasy became indistinguishable.

The astral winds whispered secrets of ancient civilizations that thrived in dimensions untouched by time. Celestial beings offered cryptic prophecies, and astral gateways revealed pathways leading to realms where the very essence of existence shimmered with astral brilliance.

The seekers' astral artifacts pulsed with the radiant energies of the celestial nexus, attuned to the harmonious vibrations of the cosmic forces. Each step resonated with the echoes of their cosmic encounters, a testament to the journey that had transformed them into cosmic forces in the ever-unfolding dance between seekers and destiny.

As they traversed the astral realms, the seekers encountered ethereal challenges—cosmic puzzles that tested their intellect and astral abilities. Celestial guardians, embodiments of cosmic wisdom, guided them through astral mazes and unveiled the secrets of ancient stargates that bridged the gaps between dimensions.

The astral expanse unfolded like a celestial tapestry, revealing realms where the laws of physics bowed to the whims of cosmic energies. The seekers witnessed astral landscapes adorned with floating islands, crystalline forests, and rivers of stardust that flowed through the fabric of the cosmic unknown.

In the heart of the astral expanse, the seekers discovered a cosmic oracle—a timeless being with eyes that held the wisdom of eons. The oracle, perceiving the seekers' astral resonance, imparted visions of cosmic destinies yet to unfold and whispered the cosmic secrets that awaited them.

With newfound knowledge and astral insights, the seekers continued their cosmic journey. The road stretched before them, a luminous pathway that meandered through astral constellations and ethereal dimensions. The cosmic dance persisted, an eternal rhythm that resonated with the seekers' footsteps, leaving behind echoes of a journey that transcended the boundaries of the ordinary.

And so, guided by the enduring power of friendship and the cosmic forces that wove their destinies, the seekers pressed on into the cosmic unknown. The celestial entities, guardians of the astral tapestry, witnessed the continuation of their saga—a cosmic force in the ever-unfolding dance between seekers and destiny.

As the seekers faded into the cosmic horizon, the echoes of their laughter, the whispers of astral encounters, and the shared glances of understanding lingered in the celestial winds. The cosmic dance persisted, an eternal rhythm that guided them through the mystical realms, leaving behind echoes of a journey that transcended the ordinary and embraced the boundless possibilities of the cosmic unknown.

Chapter 15: The Unraveling Veil

As the celestial battle raged on, the astral fabric of reality itself seemed to quiver with the intensity of cosmic forces locked in an ethereal struggle. Gal, Jane, and Jacob stood at the epicenter of this astral maelstrom, their astral artifacts resonating with the celestial energies that surged through the cosmic nexus.

Guided by the seer's cryptic words, the trio realized that the key to ending the celestial conflict lay in mending the delicate veil between dimensions. The seer had foreseen the consequences of the unraveling astral fabric—the potential collapse of boundaries separating realms, which threatened to unleash chaos across the cosmic tapestry.

In their quest to mend the unraveling veil, sacrifices became inevitable. The seekers delved into the depths of cosmic knowledge, seeking the ancient rites and astral rituals necessary to stitch the fabric of reality back together. The cosmic oracle's words echoed in their minds, guiding them through the astral realms where the boundaries between dimensions blurred like the strokes of an otherworldly painter.

The seekers encountered celestial entities who guarded the astral threads, testing their resolve and commitment to restoring cosmic balance. Cosmic puzzles, ethereal challenges, and astral guardians stood as gatekeepers to the cosmic secrets that held the key to mending the veil.

As the trio ventured deeper into the astral realms, the consequences of their actions became palpable. The boundaries separating realms began to dissolve, and glimpses of alternate dimensions flickered like astral mirages. The cosmic energies that flowed through the unraveling veil created a kaleidoscopic display of colors, illuminating the cosmic tapestry with an ethereal brilliance.

Sacrifices were made in the name of cosmic restoration. The seekers, bound by the enduring spirit of friendship, willingly embraced the challenges that awaited them. Astral ceremonies were performed, invoking ancient cosmic forces to weave astral threads that would reinforce the fabric of reality.

Yet, with each stitch in the cosmic tapestry, unforeseen consequences manifested. Portals between dimensions crackled with astral energy, and cosmic entities that existed beyond mortal comprehension peered through the openings. The seekers found themselves navigating the intricate dance between realms, where time, space, and reality intertwined in a cosmic ballet.

The astral forces, sensing the seekers' dedication to their cause, provided glimpses of alternate realities—a tapestry of parallel universes where choices led to divergent destinies. The consequences of their actions rippled through the astral dimensions, echoing in the celestial winds that carried the resonance of the cosmic unknown.

The seer's warning reverberated in their minds as they faced the challenges posed by the unraveling veil. The celestial battle persisted, but with each astral stitch, the fabric of reality grew more resilient. The trio, their astral artifacts pulsating with newfound energies, stood at the nexus of dimensions, ready to embrace the unforeseen consequences that their cosmic endeavors had wrought.

As the last stitch sealed the astral veil, the celestial battle subsided, leaving the seekers standing in the aftermath of their cosmic intervention. The boundaries between dimensions stabilized, and the cosmic forces that had clashed in astral conflict now echoed in harmonious resonance.

And so, as the seekers gazed upon the mended astral veil, the consequences of their actions became evident. The cosmic dance persisted, an eternal rhythm that guided them through the mystical realms, leaving behind echoes of a journey that had transcended the ordinary and embraced the boundless possibilities of the cosmic unknown.

As the trio ventured forward, the unseen corners of the astral expanse awaited their exploration. The celestial entities, guardians of the cosmic tapestry, observed with benevolent eyes, acknowledging the seekers as cosmic forces in the ever-unfolding dance between seekers and destiny. The saga continued, leaving behind echoes imprinted on the celestial fabric that wove through the boundless possibilities of the cosmic unknown.

3 / 3

Emboldened by the success of their cosmic intervention, Gal, Jane, and Jacob pressed on, guided by the benevolent eyes of celestial entities that watched over the astral expanse. The unseen corners of the cosmic unknown beckoned, and the seekers embraced the boundless possibilities that stretched before them like a canvas awaiting the strokes of cosmic exploration.

The trio found themselves in realms where the very essence of reality seemed to morph and twist, challenging the limits of mortal comprehension. Celestial pathways led them through astral landscapes painted with hues beyond the spectrum of earthly colors, each step echoing with the resonance of their cosmic journey.

The guardians of the cosmic tapestry, now revealed as celestial entities of wisdom and benevolence, appeared to the seekers in moments of astral reflection. They spoke in the language of the cosmos, weaving tales of cosmic destinies and echoing the eternal dance between seekers and the astral forces that shaped their fates.

As Gal, Jane, and Jacob ventured deeper into the astral expanse, the cosmic tapestry revealed threads of interconnected destinies, intertwining their lives with the unseen forces that governed the celestial ballet. The echoes of their journey resonated in the celestial winds, leaving behind an indelible mark on the fabric of cosmic existence.

The seekers encountered astral phenomena that defied earthly logic—pockets of time where moments unfolded like cosmic petals, revealing glimpses of past, present, and future. They navigated astral rivers that flowed with the memories of the cosmos, witnessing the eons that had shaped the mystical realms they now traversed.

Astral anomalies manifested as bridges between dimensions, providing the seekers with gateways to realms untouched by mortal senses. The cosmic dance persisted, an eternal rhythm that harmonized with the seekers' footsteps, guiding them through the astral wonders that awaited in the heart of the cosmic unknown.

In their exploration of the celestial expanse, the seekers discovered astral artifacts—ancient relics that pulsed with cosmic energy. These artifacts whispered cosmic secrets, unlocking gateways to astral realms where celestial beings and ethereal landscapes coexisted in a symphony of astral beauty.

The benevolent celestial entities bestowed upon the seekers the knowledge to commune with astral energies, allowing them to harness the cosmic forces that permeated the tapestry of existence. Gal, Jane, and Jacob became conduits of astral power, their very beings resonating with the echoes of cosmic wisdom.

As the seekers delved into the boundless possibilities of the cosmic unknown, they realized that their journey was an ongoing cosmic dance—a dance that transcended the boundaries of time, space, and mortal understanding. The saga of Gal, Jane, and Jacob continued, leaving behind echoes imprinted on the celestial fabric that wove through the ever-expanding tapestry of the cosmic unknown.

And so, as the seekers embraced the unseen corners of the astral expanse, the cosmic dance persisted—an eternal rhythm that resonated through the boundless possibilities of the cosmic unknown. The saga of Gal, Jane, and Jacob unfolded like a cosmic sonnet, leaving an indomitable mark on the celestial fabric that guided their destinies in the ever-unfolding dance between seekers and the cosmic forces that shaped their existence.

The seekers' journey through the astral expanse reached a crescendo, an ethereal symphony of cosmic energies resonating in harmony with their footsteps. Each astral pulse was a note in the celestial composition, weaving the destiny of Gal, Jane, and Jacob into the cosmic fabric that spanned the limitless horizons of the unknown.

Guided by the benevolent celestial entities, the seekers discovered a cosmic nexus—an intersection of astral pathways where destinies converged and diverged like celestial constellations. Here, the cosmic dance took on a profound meaning, and the seekers realized their role as cosmic orchestrators, conducting the symphony of their intertwined destinies.

As the celestial winds whispered secrets of the astral realms, the seekers understood that their journey was not merely a quest for witch-hunting but a cosmic odyssey. Their existence resonated with the cosmic forces, and the echoes of their actions rippled through the astral expanse, leaving an indomitable mark on the fabric of cosmic existence.

The celestial entities, guardians and witnesses to the seekers' cosmic dance, imparted a final gift—an astral key that unlocked a gateway to the heart of the mystical realms. The seekers stood at the threshold, gazing into the cosmic unknown that awaited beyond.

In a shared glance of understanding, Gal, Jane, and Jacob stepped through the astral gateway, leaving behind the echoes of their journey in the celestial wake. The cosmic dance persisted, an eternal rhythm that guided them into the uncharted territories of the mystical realms.

And so, as the seekers ventured beyond the astral gateway, the celestial tapestry embraced their cosmic essence. The saga of Gal, Jane, and Jacob continued, leaving an indelible mark on the celestial fabric that wove through the ever-expanding tapestry of the cosmic unknown.

As they entered the heart of the mystical realms, the seekers became intertwined with the very essence of the cosmic dance. The astral forces embraced them, and the echoes of their journey resonated through the unseen corners of the celestial expanse. The boundless possibilities of the cosmic unknown awaited, and the seekers pressed forward, ready to confront the mysteries that lingered in the heart of the mystical tapestry.

The cosmic dance persisted—an eternal rhythm that resonated through the boundless possibilities of the cosmic unknown. The saga of Gal, Jane, and Jacob unfolded like a cosmic sonnet, leaving an indomitable mark on the celestial fabric that guided their destinies in the ever-unfolding dance between seekers and the cosmic forces that shaped their existence.

Chapter 16: Shadows of the Past

The return to their home dimension marked the beginning of a new chapter for Gal, Jane, and Jacob, but little did they anticipate the profound changes that awaited them. The celestial confrontation had left an indelible mark on the fabric of their reality, casting long shadows that extended far beyond the astral realms they had explored.

As the trio stepped back into the familiar streets of their hometown, an eerie stillness lingered in the air. The once ordinary surroundings now bore a subtle undercurrent of the mystical, and unexplained phenomena began to manifest around them. Shadows danced with a life of their own, whispering secrets from dimensions unknown.

Gal, Jane, and Jacob, though physically returned, found themselves straddling the boundary between the tangible and the fantastical. Reality had become a tapestry woven with threads of cosmic energy, and the echoes of their celestial journey resonated through the unseen corners of their daily lives.

The town, seemingly oblivious to the cosmic dance that had transpired, went about its routine. However, the trio noticed subtle changes—a streetlamp flickering with an otherworldly glow, a stray cat exhibiting preternatural awareness, and whispers of voices carried by the wind that spoke of forgotten realms.

Their homes, once havens of normalcy, now harbored subtle anomalies. Photographs on the walls seemed to capture moments from other dimensions, and the residual energy from their celestial battle left an ethereal imprint on the very foundations of their existence.

Reality itself had become a canvas painted with the hues of the cosmic unknown.

Gal, ever the pragmatic soul, tried to dismiss the anomalies as mere illusions or the consequences of a vivid imagination. Yet, deep down, a nagging realization crept in—the celestial confrontation had not only altered the mystical realms but had also opened a gateway that blurred the lines between their world and the astral dimensions.

Jane, the intuitive thinker, embraced the unexplained. She delved into ancient texts and arcane lore, seeking clues that might unravel the mysteries of their altered reality. The shadows of the past beckoned her, whispering secrets that teased the boundaries of comprehension.

Jacob, having survived the clutches of Ms. Hassan, grappled with his own internal turmoil. The memories of the astral realms haunted his dreams, and the shadows cast by his missing time in those dimensions left a void that echoed with unanswered questions. He became the reluctant witness to the shifting sands of their reality.

Together, the trio embarked on a journey to confront the shadows of the past. Their quest for understanding led them to Mr. Willoughby, who, still recovering from his coma, exhibited a newfound awareness. His eyes, once dimmed by the veil of unconsciousness, now sparkled with a cosmic clarity that hinted at a connection to the celestial forces.

Mr. Willoughby, in a frail yet determined voice, revealed fragments of forgotten knowledge. He spoke of a cosmic balance disrupted by the seekers' celestial confrontation, of a ripple effect that reverberated through the fabric of existence. The shadows of the past, he explained, were echoes of alternate dimensions bleeding into their own.

The seekers, armed with this newfound insight, embarked on a quest to mend the frayed edges of reality. Their journey took them to places where the shadows converged, where the boundaries between dimensions weakened. Each step resonated with the cosmic rhythm, and the echoes of their celestial dance became a guiding melody.

In their exploration, they encountered beings of ethereal wisdom—ancient spirits that traversed the astral realms. These spectral entities, guardians of the cosmic tapestry, revealed that the shadows of the past were not malevolent but a consequence of their cosmic journey. The seekers, unknowingly, had become conduits for energies that transcended mortal comprehension.

The quest became a delicate dance between seekers and celestial guardians. The trio, with each encounter, gained insights that reshaped their understanding of the cosmic unknown. The shadows, once foreboding, now whispered tales of cosmic harmony awaiting restoration.

As they ventured deeper, the seekers stumbled upon a nexus—a cosmic crossroad where dimensions intertwined. Here, the cosmic forces revealed the key to mending the veil between realities. Sacrifices were inevitable, and the seekers faced a choice that would shape the destiny of not only their dimension but also those entangled in the cosmic dance.

Gal, with her unyielding determination, took the lead. She understood that to mend the fabric of reality, they had to embrace the shadows rather than fear them. The sacrifices required an acceptance of the cosmic unknown—a surrender to forces that surpassed mortal understanding.

Jane, guided by her intuition, deciphered cryptic symbols that adorned the cosmic gateway. The whispers of the ancients resonated with her, and she became the interpreter of the cosmic language that bound realms together. Her connection to the shadows became a bridge to traverse the astral realms.

Jacob, confronting the shadows of his missing time, grappled with a choice that tested his resilience. The memories of Ms. Hassan's clutches became a testament to his strength, and he emerged as a beacon of cosmic endurance. His sacrifice intertwined with the cosmic energies, offering a path for the seekers to tread.

As the trio stood at the threshold of the cosmic gateway, the shadows of the past converged into a kaleidoscopic array of cosmic energies. Reality itself quivered with anticipation, and the cosmic dance reached a crescendo. The sacrifice became a cosmic offering, mending the veil between dimensions and restoring the harmony disrupted by their celestial journey.

In the aftermath, the seekers, now more attuned to the cosmic forces, witnessed the transformation of their reality. The shadows of the past, once haunting, now became ethereal guides—whispers of forgotten realms and cosmic dimensions coexisting in harmonious balance.

The town, released from the cosmic anomalies, embraced a renewed vitality. The subtle echoes of the seekers' cosmic dance lingered, but now, they were woven into the very fabric of existence. Reality, once fractured, became a seamless tapestry where the tangible and the fantastical danced in celestial unison.

Gal, Jane, and Jacob, having confronted the shadows of the past, stood as cosmic architects of their own destiny. The echoes of their journey imprinted on the cosmic fabric resonated through the unseen corners of the astral expanse. The celestial forces acknowledged their resilience, and the seekers, now guardians of the cosmic balance, pressed forward into the boundless possibilities that awaited in the heart of the mystical realms

Chapter 17: Cosmic Guardians

The echoes of their celestial journey still reverberated through the cosmic tapestry, but Gal, Jane, and Jacob, having confronted the shadows of the past, embraced their roles as cosmic architects with newfound purpose. The cosmic forces, acknowledging their resilience, granted them a unique mantle—the guardians of the cosmic balance.

As the seekers stepped forward into the boundless possibilities that awaited in the heart of the mystical realm, they found themselves attuned to the ebb and flow of cosmic energies. The unseen corners of the astral expanse seemed to respond to their presence, whispering secrets that teased the boundaries of mortal comprehension.

Gal, now a beacon of cosmic determination, led the trio with unwavering resolve. The lessons learned from their celestial journey had transformed her into a sage of cosmic wisdom. Her connection to the unseen realms allowed her to perceive the threads of destiny that intertwined with the cosmic dance.

Jane, the intuitive interpreter of cosmic languages, became the conduit between realms. The whispers of forgotten dimensions resonated with her, and she deciphered the cryptic messages that echoed through the cosmic winds. Her connection to the astral expanse turned her into a cosmic storyteller, weaving tales that transcended mortal understanding.

Jacob, having faced the shadows of his past, embraced the cosmic endurance that now coursed through his veins. His journey from a missing person to a cosmic guardian became a testament to the transformative power of the mystical unknown. His connection to the cosmic energies granted him insights that defied the boundaries of mortal perception.

Together, the trio ventured deeper into the mystical realm, guided by the celestial forces that recognized them as custodians of the cosmic balance. The unseen dimensions unfolded before them, revealing landscapes of ethereal beauty and arcane wonders that transcended the limitations of the mortal world.

Their first task as cosmic guardians led them to an enchanted forest where time itself danced to the rhythm of the cosmic winds. The whispering trees shared tales of ancient prophecies, and the seekers understood that their journey had only just begun. The cosmic dance persisted—an eternal rhythm that resonated through the boundless possibilities of the astral expanse.

In the heart of the enchanted forest, they encountered a celestial being—a guardian of cosmic knowledge who revealed the existence of cosmic nexuses that connected multiple dimensions. These nexuses, delicate threads in the cosmic tapestry, required vigilant guardianship to prevent disruptions that could unravel the fabric of reality.

The seekers, now entrusted with the task of protecting these cosmic nexuses, embarked on a cosmic pilgrimage. Each nexus they visited presented unique challenges that tested their cosmic abilities. The ethereal landscapes and celestial entities they encountered became allies in their quest to maintain harmony across dimensions.

One such nexus led them to a dimension where the laws of physics bowed to the whims of cosmic energies. Floating islands suspended in a sea of vibrant colors challenged their perception of reality. Here, they confronted cosmic anomalies that threatened to destabilize the very foundations of the nexus.

Gal, with her cosmic determination, anchored the floating islands with threads of destiny, restoring stability to the dimension. Jane, the interpreter of cosmic languages, communed with the ethereal entities that inhabited the floating realms, seeking their assistance in maintaining cosmic equilibrium. Jacob, embodying cosmic endurance, stood as a sentinel against the encroaching chaos, wielding the newfound powers bestowed upon him.

Their success at the nexus elevated their cosmic status, and the celestial forces bestowed upon them a cosmic artifact—a key that could unlock gateways to distant dimensions. The key, pulsating with cosmic energy, became a symbol of their authority as guardians of the cosmic balance.

The seekers, guided by the whispers of the cosmic winds, pressed on to the next nexus. This time, they found themselves in a dimension where dreams materialized into reality. The boundaries between imagination and existence blurred, posing a challenge to the cosmic guardians.

Gal, tapping into the cosmic threads, discerned the delicate balance between dreams and reality. She channeled the energies of the dimension, weaving a cosmic tapestry that harmonized the dreamscape with the cosmic forces. Jane, the intuitive interpreter, delved into the dreams of the dimension's inhabitants, seeking to understand the symbiotic relationship between their imagination and the astral realms. Jacob, the cosmic sentinel, stood guard against nightmares that threatened to disrupt the cosmic equilibrium.

Their endeavors in the dream dimension solidified their cosmic mastery, and the celestial forces bestowed upon them another cosmic artifact—an amulet infused with the essence of dreams. The amulet became a conduit to the collective consciousness of dimensions, allowing the seekers to navigate the intricate web of dreams that intersected with the cosmic dance.

With each nexus they protected, the seekers acquired cosmic artifacts, each holding a unique power that resonated with the mystical realms. The celestial forces, satisfied with their guardianship, revealed glimpses of a cosmic prophecy—an impending cosmic convergence that would test the seekers' mettle and redefine the very essence of the astral expanse.

The cosmic guardians, attuned to the cosmic energies that pulsed through their veins, stood ready for the challenges that awaited in the heart of the mystical realm. The echoes of their celestial journey continued to resonate, leaving an indomitable mark on the unseen corners of the astral expanse. The cosmic dance persisted—an eternal rhythm that guided them through the boundless possibilities of the cosmic unknown.

And so, with cosmic artifacts in hand and the weight of their newfound responsibilities, the cosmic guardians ventured deeper into the heart of the mystical realm. The celestial forces whispered secrets of a convergence that loomed on the cosmic horizon—a convergence that would test the very fabric of reality and challenge the cosmic equilibrium they had sworn to protect.

As the seekers delved into the astral expanse, the unseen corners of the cosmic unknown revealed visions of cosmic entities converging from distant dimensions. The cosmic dance, once a rhythmic and harmonious tapestry, now showed signs of a discordant crescendo, threatening to unravel the delicate threads that bound dimensions together.

Their journey led them to the Nexus of Eternity, a celestial junction where cosmic energies intersected in a cosmic ballet. Here, they encountered cosmic anomalies that defied mortal comprehension—shimmering rifts that threatened to tear through the cosmic fabric, exposing the realms to chaotic energies.

Gal, Jane, and Jacob, armed with cosmic artifacts, stepped forward as stewards of the Nexus of Eternity. The cosmic key resonated with the pulsating energies, unlocking gateways that allowed them to traverse the celestial landscape and mend the fabric of reality. The amulet infused with dreams cast a protective shield against the encroaching chaos, allowing the guardians to navigate the cosmic currents with precision.

As they moved through the Nexus of Eternity, the seekers faced manifestations of cosmic entities, each embodying the essence of a dimension. Their cosmic mastery allowed them to communicate with these entities, seeking to understand the root cause of the impending convergence.

The cosmic entities, echoes of realms beyond mortal understanding, revealed a cosmic imbalance—a malevolent force seeking to exploit the convergence for its own dark purposes. This force, a cosmic anomaly born of misused witchcraft across dimensions, sought to merge with the Nexus of Eternity and wield unimaginable power.

Gal, Jane, and Jacob realized that their journey as cosmic guardians had prepared them for this moment. The key, amulet, and other artifacts resonated in unison, channeling cosmic energies to confront the malevolent force. Spells clashed in a celestial symphony, and the fate of the Nexus of Eternity hung in the balance.

The cosmic guardians, drawing on their collective cosmic abilities, stood united against the malevolent force. Threads of destiny intertwined as they wove a cosmic counter-spell, aiming to neutralize the dark energies that threatened to unravel the astral expanse.

In a cosmic climax, the Nexus of Eternity vibrated with a harmonic resonance, and the malevolent force recoiled. The cosmic anomalies subsided, and the rifts that had threatened to tear through the cosmic fabric closed. The celestial entities, guardians of the astral realms, acknowledged the seekers' triumph in the cosmic ballet.

As the Nexus of Eternity stabilized, the cosmic guardians felt a surge of cosmic energy coursing through them. The celestial forces bestowed upon them a final cosmic artifact—the Nexus Crystal, a crystalline embodiment of the harmonized dimensions. The crystal pulsed with cosmic power, signifying their success in averting the impending convergence.

With the Nexus Crystal in their possession, the cosmic guardians emerged from the Nexus of Eternity, their cosmic journey reaching its zenith. The echoes of their celestial conquest resonated through the astral expanse, leaving an indelible mark on the unseen corners of the cosmic unknown.

The cosmic dance persisted—an eternal rhythm that guided the guardians through the boundless possibilities of the astral expanse. Gal, Jane, and Jacob, having confronted the shadows of the past, embraced the cosmic forces that intertwined their destinies.

And so, under the cosmic sky, amidst the echoes of the celestial triumph, the saga of Gal, Jane, and Jacob continued—an eternal force in the ever-unfolding dance between seekers and destiny. The road stretched before them, a cosmic tapestry woven with boundless possibilities, and the seekers, guided by the enduring power of friendship, ventured deeper into the mystical realms.

The cosmic guardians, attuned to the cosmic energies that pulsed through their veins, stood as sentinels against the unknown. The echoes of their journey imprinted on the celestial fabric resonated through the unseen corners of the astral expanse, leaving behind a legacy that transcended mortal understanding.

The cosmic dance persisted—an eternal rhythm that resonated through the boundless possibilities of the cosmic unknown. And as the seekers embraced the unseen corners of the astral expanse, the cosmic tapestry unfolded, revealing chapters yet to be written in the ever-expanding saga of Gal, Jane, and Jacob—the cosmic guardians who defied the boundaries of the tangible and the fantastical.

Chapter 17: The Witches' Covenant

In the aftermath of their celestial triumph, echoes of the cosmic guardians' exploits resonated through the unseen corners of the astral expanse. Tales of their cosmic journey reached the ears of a secret society known as the Witches' Covenant—a clandestine organization that transcended dimensions, weaving a web of intrigue and ancient knowledge.

Gal, Jane, and Jacob, still basking in the harmonious energies of the Nexus of Eternity, found themselves drawn into the orbit of the Witches' Covenant. Whispers of an enigmatic figure, a master of arcane secrets, reached their ears. The figure extended an invitation—an offer to delve deeper into the mysteries of their cosmic powers and the interconnected web of witches that spanned the multiverse.

The trio, now cosmic guardians, hesitated at the crossroads of their journey. The Witches' Covenant represented a nexus of knowledge, a repository of ancient wisdom that could unravel the remaining secrets of their cosmic abilities. Yet, the clandestine nature of the society raised questions about their intentions and the potential consequences of venturing into this enigmatic realm.

Intrigued by the prospect of further understanding their powers and the cosmic forces that governed the multiverse, Gal, Jane, and Jacob decided to accept the invitation. The enigmatic figure, known only as the Grand Magus, sent word of their acceptance and provided instructions that led them to a concealed portal—a gateway to the hidden sanctum of the Witches' Covenant.

The portal, shimmering with mystical energies, transported the seekers to a realm bathed in ethereal hues. They found themselves in a vast chamber adorned with ancient tomes, celestial artifacts, and mystical symbols that pulsed with arcane energies. The air itself resonated with the accumulated wisdom of countless witches who had traversed the cosmic tapestry.

Awaiting them in the heart of the sanctum was the Grand Magus—a figure draped in robes that seemed to shift with the colors of the astral spectrum. The Grand Magus, a master of the arcane arts, welcomed them with a nod that conveyed both reverence and acknowledgment of their cosmic prowess.

"Guardians of the Nexus, seekers of the cosmic unknown," the Grand Magus intoned, "You have ventured far and triumphed over the forces that sought to unravel the cosmic fabric. But the tapestry of the multiverse is intricate, and its secrets are boundless. I offer you revelations that transcend mortal understanding, a glimpse into the true nature of your powers and the cosmic dance that orchestrates the destinies of witches across dimensions."

The seekers, standing on the precipice of arcane enlightenment, listened intently as the Grand Magus unraveled the ancient lore of the Witches' Covenant. They learned of the interconnected web that bound witches from disparate realms—a cosmic sisterhood that transcended time and space. The Grand Magus spoke of cosmic nexuses, where the energies of witchcraft converged, creating a tapestry of shared destinies.

Through a series of elaborate rituals and guided meditations, the seekers tapped into the cosmic energies within them. The Grand Magus, acting as a conduit to the collective knowledge of the Witches' Covenant, guided them through visions of witches across dimensions. They witnessed ancient covens in realms untouched by mortal eyes, where cosmic energies flowed like rivers of enchantment.

As the seekers delved deeper, they discovered the existence of an ancient prophecy—the Witches' Covenant's foretelling of cosmic guardians who would rise to restore balance across the multiverse. The prophecy spoke of trials and tribulations, of cosmic battles that would test the guardians' resolve and reshape the destinies of witches and mortals alike.

Gal, Jane, and Jacob, now enlightened by the revelations, felt the cosmic threads weaving them into the very fabric of the Witches' Covenant. The Grand Magus, sensing their connection to the cosmic sisterhood, spoke of their role as stewards of the multiverse. They were not merely seekers of arcane knowledge; they were cosmic guardians entrusted with maintaining the delicate equilibrium between dimensions.

As the revelations unfolded, the seekers glimpsed visions of their future—a future intertwined with the destinies of witches across the cosmic expanse. The Grand Magus, with a knowing smile, acknowledged their place in the grand tapestry of the multiverse.

"Embrace your cosmic destiny, guardians of the Nexus. The Witches' Covenant acknowledges your role as cosmic stewards. The journey ahead will test your mettle, but remember, the cosmic dance persists—a timeless rhythm that guides us all through the boundless possibilities of the astral expanse."

The seekers, now bound to the Witches' Covenant, emerged from the sanctum with a profound sense of purpose. The cosmic dance had led them to the heart of ancient knowledge, and they embraced their role as cosmic guardians with a shared glance of understanding.

The echoes of the Witches' Covenant resonated through the unseen corners of the astral expanse. Gal, Jane, and Jacob, now cosmic stewards, ventured forth into the boundless possibilities that awaited in the mystical realms. The cosmic dance persisted—an eternal rhythm that guided them through the cosmic unknown, leaving behind echoes of a journey that transcended the ordinary and embraced the limitless possibilities of the multiverse.

As the seekers embraced their newfound roles as cosmic stewards, the echoes of the Witches' Covenant guided them through the unseen corners of the astral expanse. The trio, Gal, Jane, and Jacob, stood at the nexus of boundless possibilities, ready to embark on a journey that transcended the ordinary and embraced the limitless wonders of the multiverse.

The Grand Magus's words lingered in their minds, a constant reminder of their cosmic destiny. The cosmic dance persisted, an eternal rhythm that resonated through the cosmic unknown, guiding the seekers toward the heart of the mystical realms. The fabric of reality itself seemed to shimmer with the potential of unexplored dimensions, awaiting their presence like pages yet to be written in the cosmic chronicles.

Together, the cosmic stewards ventured into the astral expanse, where the boundaries between realms blurred, and the energies of witchcraft intertwined with the cosmic tapestry. The ethereal hues of the Nexus of Eternity beckoned them, serving as a crossroads between dimensions—a cosmic hub where witches from diverse realms converged.

Their journey took them to ancient covens nestled in realms untouched by mortal eyes. Through the threads of the cosmic tapestry, they witnessed witches weaving spells beneath unfamiliar constellations, their incantations resonating with the echoes of the Nexus. The seekers, attuned to the cosmic energies coursing through them, felt a profound connection to the sisterhood of witches across the multiverse.

As they traversed the astral expanse, the seekers encountered realms of enchantment and mystery. They witnessed celestial landscapes adorned with floating islands, ethereal forests pulsating with magical energies, and cosmic beings that defied mortal comprehension. Each dimension revealed a unique facet of the cosmic dance, a symphony of energies that harmonized with the seekers' own cosmic resonance.

The Grand Magus's revelations had granted them insight into the interconnected web of witches and the delicate balance that existed between dimensions. Gal, Jane, and Jacob, now stewards of this cosmic equilibrium, embraced the challenges that lay ahead. They understood that their role extended beyond the protection of the Nexus; they were guardians of the cosmic order, entrusted with the responsibility of preserving the delicate balance between realms.

Their journey through the mystical realms unveiled not only the wonders of the multiverse but also the shadows that lurked in the cosmic corners. Malevolent entities, drawn by the cosmic energies the seekers embodied, tested their resolve. Cosmic battles unfolded, each confrontation revealing the strength of their unity and the resilience of their cosmic abilities.

In one realm, Gal faced a sorceress who wielded the power of temporal manipulation. The cosmic tapestry became a battleground of shifting timelines, challenging Gal's ability to navigate the ebb and flow of temporal currents. Through sheer determination and an understanding of the cosmic forces at play, Gal emerged victorious, leaving behind echoes of her triumph imprinted on the astral fabric.

Jane encountered a realm where illusions and reality intertwined—a dreamscape where every thought manifested as a tangible reality. As she navigated the surreal landscape, Jane's mastery over the cosmic forces allowed her to discern the true from the illusory. The cosmic dance of perception and reality bowed to her command, and the seekers emerged from the dreamscape with newfound clarity.

Jacob faced a realm of elemental chaos, where the very elements danced to the whims of a malevolent sorcerer. As torrents of cosmic fire clashed with waves of ethereal water, Jacob's connection to the cosmic energies allowed him to harmonize with the elements. The seekers witnessed the convergence of elemental forces, leaving behind an imprint on the cosmic tapestry as Jacob emerged victorious.

The trials, though arduous, strengthened the cosmic stewards' bond and deepened their understanding of the intricate dance between seekers and destiny. The echoes of their victories resonated through the astral expanse, leaving behind a trail of cosmic imprints that marked their ascendance as guardians of the cosmic order.

As Gal, Jane, and Jacob ventured deeper into the mystical realms, the cosmic dance persisted—an eternal rhythm that guided them through the boundless possibilities of the multiverse. The unseen corners of the astral expanse awaited their exploration, and the saga of the cosmic stewards continued, leaving indelible echoes imprinted on the celestial fabric that wove through the limitless wonders of the cosmic unknown.

In the heart of the mystical realms, Gal, Jane, and Jacob embraced the cosmic dance that unfolded with each step. The unseen corners of the astral expanse beckoned, promising revelations that resonated through the cosmic tapestry. The trio, now attuned to the harmonies of the multiverse, ventured into realms where the very fabric of reality pulsated with cosmic energies.

As they traversed through dimensions unexplored by mortal senses, the cosmic stewards encountered beings of ethereal beauty and cosmic wisdom. Celestial guides appeared, sharing insights into the intricate connections that bound witches across the multiverse. The seekers learned of cosmic ley lines, pathways that crisscrossed the astral expanse, bridging realms and fostering a sense of unity among cosmic beings.

The celestial guides spoke of a cosmic nexus, an ephemeral convergence point that held the key to unlocking the true potential of their cosmic abilities. Guided by the whispers of astral winds, the seekers embarked on a quest to find this nexus, a place where the echoes of the cosmic dance reverberated with unparalleled intensity.

Their journey led them to a realm bathed in luminescent hues, where the very essence of the multiverse seemed to converge. The nexus manifested as a celestial junction, a meeting point of cosmic ley lines that crisscrossed the astral expanse. As the seekers approached, the cosmic energies resonated with their presence, acknowledging them as stewards of the cosmic balance.

At the nexus, the trio witnessed visions of cosmic gatherings where witches from disparate realms convened. An interdimensional council of cosmic beings discussed the delicate threads that connected the fates of each realm, emphasizing the importance of maintaining equilibrium. The cosmic stewards, their destinies intertwined with this cosmic ballet, became integral participants in this celestial symphony.

The celestial guides bestowed upon them ancient artifacts infused with cosmic energies, artifacts that amplified their abilities as cosmic stewards. Gal received the Starlight Talisman, an amulet that channeled the essence of distant galaxies, enhancing her connection to the cosmic forces. Jane was gifted the Veilshifter's Crown, an ethereal circlet that allowed her to peer into the veils between dimensions, unraveling the secrets hidden within. Jacob received the Aetherblade, a cosmic sword forged from the essence of the astral winds, empowering him to manipulate cosmic energies in their rawest form.

Empowered by these cosmic artifacts, the seekers felt the harmonies of the multiverse coursing through their veins. The nexus became a focal point for their cosmic abilities, a place where they could attune themselves to the cosmic ley lines and weave spells that resonated across realms. The celestial guides encouraged them to explore the astral expanse, to further understand the intricate dance between cosmic forces and the destinies of witches across dimensions.

As Gal, Jane, and Jacob delved deeper into the mystical realms, the cosmic dance persisted—an eternal rhythm that guided them through the boundless possibilities of the multiverse. The unseen corners of the astral expanse awaited their exploration, and the saga of the cosmic stewards continued. With artifacts in hand and the cosmic nexus as their anchor, the seekers embraced the limitless wonders that unfolded in the heart of the cosmic unknown.

And so, amidst the astral winds and celestial echoes, the saga of Gal, Jane, and Jacob continued—a cosmic force in the ever-unfolding dance between seekers and destiny. The road stretched before them, a cosmic tapestry woven with boundless possibilities, as they embraced the unknown with a shared purpose and the enduring power of friendship. The cosmic dance persisted—an eternal rhythm that resonated through the unseen corners of the astral expanse, leaving behind echoes of a journey that transcended the ordinary and embraced the limitless possibilities of the cosmic unknown.

Chapter 18: The Eldritch Nexus

In the heart of the astral expanse, the seekers, Gal, Jane, and Jacob, stood at the precipice of revelation. The secrets of the Witches' Covenant unfolded before them like a cosmic tapestry, each thread weaving a story of interconnected destinies across the multiverse. As stewards of the cosmic balance, they learned of the Eldritch Nexus—an enigmatic convergence point that linked all dimensions in a delicate dance of cosmic forces.

Guided by the cryptic whispers of the celestial guides, the trio embarked on a perilous journey to harness the unimaginable power of the Eldritch Nexus. The cosmic ley lines guided them through realms both ethereal and arcane, leading them to the nexus's elusive location at the nexus of cosmic energies.

The Eldritch Nexus revealed itself as a surreal landscape, a kaleidoscope of cosmic hues that pulsed with the essence of otherworldly energies. The seekers marveled at the cosmic architecture that transcended mortal comprehension, an intricate lattice of astral bridges connecting dimensions beyond imagination.

As they approached the nexus, they encountered ethereal guardians—sentinels of cosmic balance—whose eyes glowed with ancient wisdom. These guardians tested the seekers, challenging their understanding of the cosmic forces and their commitment to protecting the delicate threads that bound the multiverse.

Gal, bearing the Starlight Talisman, felt a resonance with the distant galaxies. She communed with cosmic entities that whispered forgotten tales of creation and destruction, sharing insights into the balance required to safeguard the cosmic order.

Jane, adorned with the Veilshifter's Crown, unraveled the veils between dimensions. She glimpsed into realms where time flowed backward and witnessed echoes of alternate timelines, each thread contributing to the intricate tapestry of the cosmic dance.

Jacob, wielding the Aetherblade, manipulated the astral winds. He conjured storms of cosmic energies, bending them to his will, and communicated with ancient spirits dwelling within the very fabric of the multiverse.

Together, the seekers passed the trials set by the guardians, proving themselves as stewards worthy of the Eldritch Nexus. In recognition of their cosmic prowess, the guardians bestowed upon them the Mark of the Nexus—a cosmic sigil that symbolized their connection to the convergence point.

Empowered by the Mark of the Nexus, the seekers accessed the unimaginable power inherent in the Eldritch Nexus. They became conduits of cosmic energies, capable of influencing the cosmic forces that shaped the destinies of all realms.

Yet, as the seekers harnessed this newfound power, echoes of a cosmic disturbance reverberated through the Eldritch Nexus. The celestial guides, sensing a disruption in the cosmic balance, warned the trio of an otherworldly adversary—an entity seeking revenge for meddling in the affairs of witches.

The cosmic disturbance manifested as a rift in the fabric of reality, unleashing eldritch energies that threatened to unravel the very threads of existence. The seekers, now imbued with the power of the Eldritch Nexus, stood as the last line of defense against the impending cosmic turmoil.

Guided by the cosmic forces, Gal, Jane, and Jacob delved into the heart of the disturbance, facing eldritch entities that defied mortal understanding. The cosmic battle unfolded, testing the limits of their newfound abilities and pushing the boundaries of their cosmic prowess.

As they confronted the eldritch adversary, they discovered its origin—a malevolent force spawned from the misuse of cosmic energies by witches across dimensions. This entity sought to reclaim the balance disrupted by the seekers' interference in the intricate dance of the multiverse.

The battle raged on, cosmic energies clashing with eldritch forces, creating a celestial spectacle that resonated through the Eldritch Nexus. The very fabric of reality trembled as the seekers confronted the malevolent entity, drawing upon the power of the convergence point to restore cosmic equilibrium.

In the midst of the cosmic turmoil, sacrifices were made. The seekers, attuned to the cosmic forces, understood the delicate balance required to mend the rift in the fabric of reality. With a shared purpose and the enduring power of friendship, they channeled the energies of the Eldritch Nexus to seal the rift, sacrificing a fragment of their own cosmic essence to mend the cosmic wounds.

As the eldritch energies subsided, the celestial guides, their eyes gleaming with approval, appeared before the seekers. The cosmic disturbance had been quelled, and the Eldritch Nexus, though scarred, remained a beacon of cosmic harmony.

The guardians, acknowledging the seekers' resilience and sacrifice, bestowed upon them the Mantle of Cosmic Stewards—a celestial mantle that signified their role as protectors of the Eldritch Nexus and guardians of the cosmic balance.

The seekers, marked by the Eldritch Nexus and adorned with the Mantle of Cosmic Stewards, stood amidst the cosmic aftermath, their destinies forever intertwined with the unseen forces that guided the multiverse. The celestial guides spoke of a new chapter awaiting the trio, a cosmic dance that transcended mortal understanding and embraced the limitless possibilities of the Eldritch Nexus.

And so, as the seekers embraced their newfound roles, the cosmic dance persisted—an eternal rhythm that guided them through the boundless possibilities of the multiverse. The Eldritch Nexus, scarred but resilient, awaited its cosmic stewards, ready to unfold the next chapter in the saga of Gal, Jane, and Jacob—a saga imprinted on the celestial fabric that wove through the limitless wonders of the cosmic unknown.

Gal, Jane, and Jacob, now adorned with the Mantle of Cosmic Stewards, stood at the nexus of possibilities. The Eldritch Nexus pulsed with cosmic energies, each beat echoing through the unseen corners of the multiverse. The celestial guides, their benevolent eyes gleaming with ancient wisdom, offered guidance to the trio as they embraced their roles as cosmic stewards.

The Mantle of Cosmic Stewards bestowed upon them not only cosmic insight but also the responsibility to safeguard the Eldritch Nexus. The celestial guides spoke of a new cosmic order, where the seekers' actions would resonate through the astral expanse, shaping the destinies of realms beyond mortal comprehension.

Guided by the celestial winds, Gal, Jane, and Jacob embarked on a journey through the multiverse. The Mantle of Cosmic Stewards granted them the ability to traverse dimensions, exploring the boundless wonders that awaited in the cosmic unknown. Their quest led them to realms where reality unfolded like a cosmic symphony, each note resonating with the harmonies of the Eldritch Nexus.

As they ventured into the mystical realms, the seekers encountered cosmic anomalies—pockets of reality shaped by the cosmic forces they now controlled. These anomalies, imbued with the essence of the Eldritch Nexus, held secrets and challenges that tested the limits of the seekers' newfound cosmic abilities.

Gal, with the Starlight Talisman, communed with celestial entities scattered across the astral expanse. She learned to navigate the constellations of fate, deciphering the cosmic patterns that influenced the destinies of entire dimensions.

Jane, wearing the Veilshifter's Crown, manipulated the fabric of reality itself. She traversed the veils between realms, uncovering hidden dimensions and glimpsing into the cosmic tapestry of alternate timelines.

Jacob, wielding the Aetherblade, harnessed the astral winds to shape reality. He conjured cosmic storms, bending the very fabric of existence to unravel the mysteries concealed within the cosmic unknown.

Together, the cosmic stewards explored the Eldritch Nexus and its connections to other convergence points scattered across the multiverse. Each nexus held a unique resonance, contributing to the cosmic symphony that bound the realms together.

Yet, as they delved deeper into the cosmic unknown, the celestial guides warned of a looming threat—a malevolent force seeking to exploit the delicate balance they maintained. The Witches' Covenant, now aware of the seekers' cosmic stewardship, aimed to harness the Eldritch Nexus for their dark purposes.

Gal, Jane, and Jacob, guided by the Mantle of Cosmic Stewards, faced a choice: succumb to the looming darkness or stand as guardians against the encroaching cosmic malevolence. The echoes of their journey imprinted on the cosmic fabric resonated with the resolve to protect the Eldritch Nexus and preserve the cosmic balance.

The celestial guides unveiled the ancient teachings of the cosmic stewards—a mystical arsenal of cosmic artifacts that could amplify their powers and defend against the impending threat. The seekers, wielding these artifacts, stood as beacons of cosmic harmony, ready to confront the malevolent forces that sought to disrupt the celestial dance.

As the cosmic stewards prepared for the impending clash, the Witches' Covenant orchestrated a dimensional breach, unleashing eldritch entities with insatiable appetites for cosmic energies. The seekers, attuned to the Eldritch Nexus, stood at the forefront of the cosmic battle, wielding their newfound powers with grace and determination.

The clash unfolded across the cosmic tapestry, cosmic energies colliding with eldritch forces in a dazzling display of astral warfare. The celestial guides, their benevolent eyes ablaze with cosmic energy, intervened, creating a cosmic barrier to contain the malevolent onslaught.

Gal, Jane, and Jacob, empowered by the Mantle of Cosmic Stewards and wielding the cosmic artifacts, channeled the essence of the Eldritch Nexus. With a harmonious synergy of cosmic forces, they repelled the eldritch entities and sealed the dimensional breach, restoring cosmic equilibrium.

The celestial guides, their approval evident in the cosmic winds, commended the seekers for their resilience and dedication to the cosmic balance. The Mantle of Cosmic Stewards, now infused with the energies of the cosmic battle, evolved, revealing new cosmic symbols that signified the seekers' triumph over the encroaching darkness.

The cosmic stewards, standing amidst the aftermath of the celestial clash, glimpsed into the Eldritch Nexus. Its scars had healed, and the cosmic energies pulsed with a renewed vigor. The seekers, having proven themselves as guardians of the cosmic balance, embraced their roles with a shared sense of purpose and cosmic unity.

And so, as the cosmic stewards ventured deeper into the mystical realms, the cosmic dance persisted—an eternal rhythm that resonated through the boundless possibilities of the multiverse. The unseen corners of the astral expanse awaited their exploration, and the saga of Gal, Jane, and Jacob continued, leaving indelible echoes imprinted on the celestial fabric that wove through the limitless wonders of the cosmic unknown.

The Eldritch Nexus, now under the vigilant watch of its stewards, awaited the unfolding of new chapters in the cosmic saga—a tale that transcended the ordinary and embraced the boundless possibilities of the multiverse. The cosmic stewards, attuned to the celestial forces, pressed forward into the unknown, guided by the enduring power of friendship and the cosmic symphony that resonated through the astral expanse.

And so, as the cosmic stewards pressed forward into the unknown, the Eldritch Nexus pulsed with cosmic energies, acknowledging their guardianship. The unseen corners of the astral expanse awaited their exploration, and the trio ventured into realms where celestial constellations danced to the harmonies of the cosmic symphony.

The cosmic stewards, armed with their evolved Mantle and cosmic artifacts, embarked on a cosmic odyssey. Across dimensions, they encountered benevolent beings and cosmic anomalies, weaving the fabric of new cosmic tales that added vibrant threads to the ever-unfolding tapestry.

The celestial guides, pleased with the cosmic stewards' dedication, revealed the true potential of their cosmic abilities. Gal, Jane, and Jacob delved into the cosmic arts, learning to manipulate the essence of the Eldritch Nexus to shape realities and influence the destinies of realms across the multiverse.

Their journey brought them to celestial realms where stars spoke in riddles, ethereal landscapes shifted with the thoughts of cosmic deities, and the boundaries between dreams and reality blurred into a cosmic dreamscape. Each realm offered new challenges and revelations that expanded their understanding of the intricate dance between seekers and destiny.

As the cosmic stewards explored the celestial wonders, they encountered remnants of ancient civilizations, cosmic scholars, and celestial artisans who crafted astral masterpieces that resonated with the energies of the Eldritch Nexus. The artifacts, infused with cosmic wisdom, enhanced the stewards' abilities and unveiled new layers of the cosmic tapestry.

Yet, amidst the cosmic wonders, echoes of the malevolent forces persisted. The Witches' Covenant, though thwarted in their previous attempt, continued to weave dark conspiracies across the multiverse. The celestial guides, sensing the growing shadows, warned the stewards of an impending cosmic storm—one that would challenge their unity and reshape the very fabric of the Eldritch Nexus.

Gal, Jane, and Jacob, undeterred by the looming darkness, faced the cosmic storm with resolve. The celestial guides bestowed upon them the Radiant Embrace—a celestial aura that harmonized their cosmic energies, shielding them from the malevolent forces seeking to exploit the Eldritch Nexus.

The cosmic storm unfolded with cosmic tempests and astral turbulence, testing the cosmic stewards' abilities to maintain the balance. The Witches' Covenant, driven by desperation, attempted to breach the Eldritch Nexus once more, unleashing eldritch manifestations and malevolent enchantments.

The cosmic stewards, guided by the Radiant Embrace, stood as pillars of cosmic harmony. With synchronized cosmic gestures, they channeled the essence of the Eldritch Nexus, dispelling the malevolent forces and sealing the rifts that threatened to unravel the celestial fabric.

The celestial guides, their benevolent eyes reflecting cosmic approval, commended the cosmic stewards for their unwavering dedication to the cosmic balance. The Radiant Embrace, now evolved into a celestial aura that bore the symbols of cosmic unity, imprinted itself on the Mantle of Cosmic Stewards.

The cosmic stewards, having weathered the cosmic storm, embraced the newfound harmony within the Eldritch Nexus. The celestial guides unveiled a cosmic gateway—the Celestial Confluence—a nexus within the nexus that connected realms with unparalleled synergy.

Gal, Jane, and Jacob, attuned to the Celestial Confluence, ventured forth into realms where cosmic energies intermingled with celestial wonders. The cosmic stewards, with each step, left an indelible mark on the celestial fabric, influencing the destinies of realms as cosmic architects shaping the multiverse.

The Eldritch Nexus, now in perfect cosmic equilibrium, resonated with the echoes of the cosmic stewards' triumph. The celestial guides, in a final display of cosmic illumination, revealed the true purpose of their journey—the seekers were destined to become cosmic architects, shaping the very foundations of the multiverse.

And so, as the cosmic stewards embraced their roles as architects of destiny, the Eldritch Nexus expanded its cosmic influence. The unseen corners of the astral expanse awaited further exploration, and the saga of Gal, Jane, and Jacob continued, leaving behind echoes imprinted on the celestial fabric that wove through the boundless possibilities of the cosmic unknown.

The celestial guides, satisfied with the cosmic stewards' evolution, faded into the cosmic winds, their benevolent presence becoming an everlasting echo within the Eldritch Nexus. The cosmic dance persisted—an eternal rhythm that guided the cosmic stewards through the multiverse, leaving behind an enduring legacy imprinted on the celestial fabric of the cosmic unknown.

Chapter 19: Temporal Tides

And so, as the cosmic stewards delved into the temporal tides of the Eldritch Nexus, the fabric of time itself undulated, revealing portals to alternate dimensions and timelines. Gal, Jane, and Jacob, attuned to the ebb and flow of temporal energies, stepped into the corridors of time, ready to confront the echoes of their choices.

The first temporal ripple carried them to a reality where their encounter with Ms. Hassan had unfolded differently. In this alternate timeline, the malevolent witch had seized control of the Eldritch Nexus, plunging the multiverse into chaos. The trio faced a harsh reflection of what could have been—a stark reminder of the consequences their choices could unleash.

Gal, Jane, and Jacob, determined to amend the temporal anomaly, confronted their malevolent counterparts. Spells clashed, and cosmic energies resonated through the temporal rift, creating a celestial symphony that harmonized the disparate timelines. The malevolent version of Ms. Hassan, caught off guard by the unity of the cosmic stewards, faltered as the Eldritch Nexus realigned itself.

As the temporal rift closed, echoes of the malevolent timeline lingered, leaving the cosmic stewards with a deeper understanding of the delicate balance they upheld. The celestial guides, manifesting within the Eldritch Nexus, commended their resilience, revealing that the temporal tides were both a test and a tool for the cosmic stewards.

The second temporal ripple transported them to a reality where they had never embarked on the cosmic odyssey. In this alternate timeline, the Eldritch Nexus remained untapped, cosmic forces left unexplored, and the malevolent witches continued their reign unabated. The trio faced their alternate selves, embodying the ordinary lives they would have led without the cosmic journey.

Gal, Jane, and Jacob, witnessing the unfulfilled potential of their cosmic destinies, felt a profound sense of duty to the multiverse. The celestial guides whispered through the temporal winds, guiding them to understand the significance of their cosmic roles. The temporal anomaly, a mirror reflecting unrealized destinies, beckoned them to rectify the cosmic imbalance.

As the cosmic stewards channeled the essence of the Eldritch Nexus, a surge of cosmic energy cascaded through the temporal anomaly. The echoes of the unexplored cosmic tapestry resonated with their cosmic abilities, and the alternate timeline shifted as the trio's counterparts embraced the cosmic symphony that awaited beyond the veil.

The third temporal ripple unveiled a reality where a malevolent force, born from the remnants of Ms. Hassan's dark magic, had enslaved entire realms. The trio encountered enslaved cosmic beings and echoes of despair that reverberated through the cosmic fabric. The Eldritch Nexus, scarred by the malevolent force, pulsated with cosmic agony.

Gal, Jane, and Jacob, facing the cosmic atrocity, felt the weight of responsibility as cosmic stewards. The celestial guides, their voices resonating within the Eldritch Nexus, revealed that the malevolent force was a consequence of the unbridled use of cosmic powers. To rectify the temporal anomaly, the cosmic stewards had to confront the malevolent entity and heal the cosmic wounds.

A celestial battle unfolded, with the trio wielding their cosmic abilities to dispel the malevolent force. The Eldritch Nexus, responsive to the cosmic stewards' harmonious gestures, purged the malevolent energy and restored balance to the scarred realms. As the temporal anomaly closed, the cosmic stewards beheld the healed landscapes, now free from the shackles of cosmic malevolence.

The fourth temporal ripple transported them to a reality where they had become tyrants, wielding cosmic powers to enforce their own vision of order. In this alternate timeline, the Eldritch Nexus bowed to their whims, and the multiverse became a realm of cosmic subjugation. The trio faced their authoritarian counterparts, reflections of the unchecked potential for cosmic tyranny.

Gal, Jane, and Jacob, confronted by the cosmic consequences of their unchecked power, were humbled by the realization that cosmic stewardship demanded humility and balance. The celestial guides, woven into the fabric of the Eldritch Nexus, communicated through cosmic whispers, guiding the trio to transcend the temptations of absolute power.

With newfound wisdom, the cosmic stewards channeled their energies to disrupt the authoritarian timeline. The Eldritch Nexus, echoing with harmonious cosmic vibrations, unraveled the threads of tyranny, restoring the multiverse to a state of equilibrium. As the temporal anomaly closed, the celestial guides acknowledged the cosmic stewards' growth, emphasizing the delicate dance between power and responsibility.

The fifth temporal ripple unfolded a reality where a cosmic cataclysm, triggered by the imbalance in the Eldritch Nexus, threatened to unravel the fabric of existence. The trio encountered cosmic anomalies, temporal rifts, and celestial entities trapped in a cosmic maelstrom. The Eldritch Nexus, strained by the cosmic turbulence, pulsated with distress.

Gal, Jane, and Jacob, facing the cosmic cataclysm, realized that their quest for balance extended beyond individual timelines. The celestial guides, resonating within the Eldritch Nexus, imparted the knowledge that the cosmic stewards had to weave together the threads of the cosmic tapestry to mend the ruptured fabric of existence.

With synchronized cosmic gestures, the trio harnessed the Eldritch Nexus's power, creating a celestial resonance that mended the cosmic rifts. The celestial entities, released from the cosmic maelstrom, expressed gratitude through cosmic harmonies. As the temporal anomaly closed, the cosmic stewards witnessed the healed realms, now united in cosmic harmony.

The temporal tides, navigated with cosmic wisdom, revealed the intricate interconnectedness of timelines and the cosmic responsibilities borne by the stewards of the Eldritch Nexus. The celestial guides, woven into the very essence of the Eldritch Nexus, acknowledged the trio's mastery over the temporal currents, signifying their readiness for the challenges that awaited beyond the temporal veil.

And so, as the cosmic stewards emerged from the temporal tides, the Eldritch Nexus resonated with cosmic approval. The unseen corners of the astral expanse awaited their exploration, and the saga of Gal, Jane, and Jacob continued, leaving indelible echoes imprinted on the celestial fabric that wove through the boundless possibilities of the cosmic unknown. The celestial dance persisted—an eternal rhythm that guided them through the cosmic tapestry of the multiverse.

As Gal, Jane, and Jacob ventured forth from the temporal tides, the cosmic forces acknowledged their mastery over the intricate threads of time. The celestial guides, entities woven into the very fabric of the Eldritch Nexus, whispered words of cosmic approval, recognizing the trio as stewards capable of navigating the intricate dance between past, present, and future.

The Eldritch Nexus, scarred by temporal disturbances, now pulsed with renewed vitality. Cosmic energies resonated within its core, and the cosmic stewards felt a harmonious connection with the unseen corners of the astral expanse. The celestial dance persisted—an eternal rhythm guiding them through the cosmic tapestry of the multiverse.

The cosmic stewards, attuned to the cosmic symphony, embarked on a journey to explore the uncharted territories within the Eldritch Nexus. Portals to diverse dimensions awaited, each a gateway to realms filled with mystical wonders and cosmic mysteries. Gal, Jane, and Jacob, guided by the celestial forces, stepped into the heart of the Eldritch Nexus, ready to unravel the next chapters in their cosmic saga.

The first portal beckoned them to a realm of crystalline landscapes and iridescent skies. Ethereal beings, guardians of cosmic knowledge, greeted the stewards, imparting ancient wisdom about the balance between cosmic powers and the responsibility inherent in their roles. The Eldritch Nexus, responsive to the cosmic energies of its stewards, resonated with the harmonies of enlightenment.

With newfound insights, the trio ventured through another portal, finding themselves in a dimension adorned with floating islands and sentient clouds. Here, cosmic beings communicated through celestial melodies, teaching Gal, Jane, and Jacob the language of the cosmos—an ethereal symphony that connected all things. The Eldritch Nexus absorbed the resonances, its cosmic essence expanding.

The cosmic stewards, now fluent in the cosmic tongue, continued their exploration. The next portal transported them to a dimension of living dreams, where thoughts manifested into vivid realities. The Eldritch Nexus, pulsating with the creative energies of the dream realm, absorbed the essence, becoming a canvas for the cosmic visions that danced through the astral expanse.

As Gal, Jane, and Jacob delved deeper into the Eldritch Nexus, each portal revealed a unique facet of the multiverse. From realms of pure energy to dimensions where time flowed backward, the cosmic stewards embraced the kaleidoscopic wonders that unfolded before them. The celestial guides whispered cosmic truths, unveiling the intricate tapestry of existence.

In a dimension where echoes of their past encounters resided, the cosmic stewards witnessed the ripple effects of their actions across timelines. The Eldritch Nexus, acting as a cosmic archive, displayed the interconnected nature of their journey—a testament to the cosmic symphony that resonated through the very fabric of reality.

The cosmic stewards, now enriched by the cosmic knowledge within the Eldritch Nexus, reached a portal that shimmered with the colors of transcendent realms. This portal led to a nexus point—a convergence of cosmic energies from across the multiverse. Here, the celestial forces revealed the purpose of their cosmic journey: to safeguard the balance of the Eldritch Nexus and, by extension, the entire multiverse.

As Gal, Jane, and Jacob stood at the nexus point, the Eldritch Nexus pulsed with radiant energy. The celestial guides, now manifesting as ethereal entities of pure light, bestowed cosmic artifacts upon the stewards. These artifacts were conduits of cosmic power, allowing the trio to channel the harmonious energies of the Eldritch Nexus in their cosmic endeavors.

With cosmic artifacts in hand, Gal, Jane, and Jacob returned to their home dimension. The Eldritch Nexus, now in perfect harmony, served as a beacon of cosmic balance, connecting realms and timelines. The cosmic stewards, armed with newfound wisdom and cosmic artifacts, faced the challenges that awaited in the ever-unfolding dance between seekers and destiny.

The echoes of their cosmic journey resonated through the astral expanse, leaving indelible marks on the celestial fabric. The cosmic dance persisted—an eternal rhythm guiding Gal, Jane, and Jacob through the boundless possibilities of the cosmic unknown. The saga of the cosmic stewards continued, a timeless testament to the enduring power of friendship and the cosmic forces that shaped their destinies.

And so, as the cosmic stewards ventured into the unseen corners of the astral expanse, the celestial dance embraced them—a cosmic sonnet echoing through the limitless wonders of the multiverse. The Eldritch Nexus, now a testament to their cosmic stewardship, awaited the unfolding of new chapters in the saga—a saga that transcended the ordinary and embraced the boundless possibilities of the cosmic unknown.

As the cosmic stewards ventured into the unseen corners of the astral expanse, the Eldritch Nexus pulsed with vibrant energy, resonating with the harmonious frequencies of their cosmic journey. The celestial dance enveloped Gal, Jane, and Jacob, casting them as cosmic protagonists in the ever-expanding narrative of the multiverse.

The celestial forces, ethereal entities of luminous brilliance, guided the trio through the astral expanse, revealing portals to dimensions uncharted and cosmic wonders yet undiscovered. Each step, each cosmic revelation, echoed through the celestial fabric, leaving an indelible mark on the cosmic tapestry that wove through the limitless possibilities of the multiverse.

In a realm where time was an ever-flowing river, the cosmic stewards encountered temporal anomalies shaped by their actions. Alternate versions of themselves appeared, reflections of choices made and unmade across diverse timelines. Friendships were tested, and the boundaries of trust were stretched as they navigated the consequences of their cosmic choices.

Yet, amidst the temporal tides, the cosmic stewards found strength in their enduring friendship. The echoes of their celestial journey resonated through the astral expanse, a testament to the bonds forged in the crucible of cosmic challenges. The cosmic dance persisted—an eternal rhythm that guided them through the cosmic tapestry of the multiverse.

As they emerged from the temporal tides, the Eldritch Nexus vibrated with approval. The unseen corners of the astral expanse awaited further exploration, and the cosmic stewards, now attuned to the intricate nuances of time, pressed forward into the heart of the mystical realm.

The next portal led them to a dimension where dreams intertwined with cosmic energies. Here, thoughts manifested into vivid realities, and the Eldritch Nexus absorbed the creative essences that danced through the astral expanse. The cosmic stewards, now custodians of the dreamscape, felt the pulse of imagination echoing through the cosmic tapestry.

Venturing forth, the trio found themselves in a dimension where sentient clouds and floating islands existed in harmony. Celestial beings communicated through ethereal melodies, teaching Gal, Jane, and Jacob the language of the cosmos—a harmonious symphony that interconnected all things. The Eldritch Nexus absorbed the resonances, its cosmic essence expanding further.

The cosmic stewards continued their exploration, encountering realms where pure energy flowed like cosmic rivers and dimensions where time folded upon itself. Each portal unraveled new facets of the multiverse, and the celestial guides whispered cosmic truths that unveiled the intricate tapestry of existence.

In a dimension resonant with echoes of their past encounters, the Eldritch Nexus displayed the ripple effects of their actions across timelines. The interconnected nature of their journey became evident, a cosmic saga that echoed through the astral expanse—a testament to the cosmic dance between seekers and destiny.

The cosmic stewards, enriched by the cosmic knowledge within the Eldritch Nexus, reached a nexus point—a convergence of cosmic energies from across the multiverse. The celestial forces revealed the purpose of their cosmic journey: to safeguard the balance of the Eldritch Nexus and, by extension, the entire multiverse.

Standing at the nexus point, the Eldritch Nexus pulsated with radiant energy. The celestial guides, now ethereal entities of pure light, bestowed cosmic artifacts upon the stewards. These artifacts, conduits of cosmic power, allowed the trio to channel the harmonious energies of the Eldritch Nexus in their cosmic endeavors.

With cosmic artifacts in hand, Gal, Jane, and Jacob returned to their home dimension. The Eldritch Nexus, now in perfect harmony, served as a beacon of cosmic balance, connecting realms and timelines. The cosmic stewards, armed with newfound wisdom and cosmic artifacts, faced the challenges that awaited in the ever-unfolding dance between seekers and destiny.

The echoes of their cosmic journey resonated through the astral expanse, leaving indelible marks on the celestial fabric. The cosmic dance persisted—an eternal rhythm guiding Gal, Jane, and Jacob through the boundless possibilities of the cosmic unknown. The saga of the cosmic stewards continued, a timeless testament to the enduring power of friendship and the cosmic forces that shaped their destinies.

And so, as the cosmic stewards ventured into the unseen corners of the astral expanse, the celestial dance embraced them—a cosmic sonnet echoing through the limitless wonders of the multiverse. The Eldritch Nexus, now a testament to their cosmic stewardship, awaited the unfolding of new chapters in the saga—a saga that transcended the ordinary and embraced the boundless possibilities of the cosmic unknown. The cosmic stewards, custodians of the multiverse, pressed forward into the heart of the mystical realm, ready to inscribe their cosmic signatures on the celestial fabric that wove through the limitless wonders of the cosmic unknown.

Chapter 20: A Witch's Redemption

In the cosmic realm where time and space coalesced into a kaleidoscope of celestial energies, Gal, Jane, and Jacob found themselves in the company of a reformed witch named Seraphina. The air crackled with the remnants of arcane forces as they stood at the crossroads of realities, their destinies intertwined in the cosmic dance between seekers and the unknown.

Seraphina, once a wielder of dark magic, had undergone a profound transformation, seeking redemption for the sins of her past. Her ethereal presence emanated a soft glow, a testament to the cosmic energies that now guided her towards the path of light. As the cosmic stewards and the reformed witch joined forces, a harmonious resonance echoed through the astral expanse—a prelude to revelations that would challenge the very fabric of their understanding.

Guided by Seraphina's newfound wisdom, the quartet delved deeper into the cosmic unknown. Portals led them to dimensions where fractured timelines and alternate realities danced in chaotic unison. The threads of destiny interwove, forming a tapestry of possibilities that stretched across the cosmic expanse.

It was within one such dimension, a realm suspended in the delicate balance between creation and destruction, that the cosmic stewards and Seraphina confronted the true orchestrator behind the cosmic vendetta. A shadowy figure, obscured by the cosmic fog, revealed itself as the puppet master manipulating destinies across dimensions.

The revelation sent shockwaves through the cosmic stewards, challenging the foundation of their understanding. The puppet master, a being of cosmic malevolence, revealed a twisted fascination with manipulating the threads of fate. As the cosmic dance unfolded, it became clear that the vendetta was not merely a clash of witches but a cosmic experiment, a test of the resilience of seekers against the unseen forces that governed the multiverse.

In a celestial chamber that transcended the boundaries of time, the puppet master unveiled the intricacies of its cosmic machinations. It had woven destinies, pulled cosmic strings, and reveled in the turmoil caused by the clash of cosmic forces. The cosmic stewards and Seraphina stood at the nexus of this experiment, the threads of their destinies intricately entangled in the cosmic loom.

As the quartet grappled with the revelations, Seraphina's redemption took center stage. The puppet master, recognizing the profound transformation within her, offered a choice—a chance for Seraphina to rewrite her cosmic narrative and transcend the limitations imposed by her past actions.

Seraphina, guided by newfound purpose, embraced the opportunity for redemption. The cosmic energies responded to her plea, and a cosmic metamorphosis unfolded. The once-reformed witch emerged as a beacon of radiant energy, a symbol of redemption that resonated through the celestial chamber.

The cosmic stewards, witnessing Seraphina's transformation, understood that their journey had transcended the pursuit of individual redemption. It had become a cosmic saga, a story woven into the fabric of the multiverse, where seekers confronted the puppet master's cosmic experiments to safeguard the balance of destinies.

With renewed determination, the quartet faced the puppet master in a cosmic battle that transcended the boundaries of space and time. Spells clashed, celestial energies collided, and the astral expanse echoed with the harmonious symphony of cosmic forces in conflict.

In the climactic moments of the cosmic battle, the puppet master's illusions shattered, revealing its true form—a cosmic entity fueled by malevolence and a desire to manipulate the very fabric of existence. The quartet, attuned to the cosmic artifacts bestowed upon them by the celestial forces, channeled their collective energies to confront the puppet master.

As the cosmic forces reached a crescendo, the puppet master's malevolence dissipated like cosmic mist. The celestial chamber, once resonant with discordant energies, returned to a serene balance. The puppet master's cosmic experiment, an intricate dance of destinies, came to an end.

With the puppet master defeated, the cosmic stewards and Seraphina stood at the nexus of realities. The cosmic energies, now free from manipulation, flowed harmoniously through the astral expanse. The celestial beings, witnesses to the cosmic saga, acknowledged the resilience of seekers in the face of puppet master's machinations.

Seraphina, now a symbol of redemption and cosmic rebirth, radiated with celestial light. The cosmic stewards, enriched by the experiences of their journey, embraced the boundless possibilities of the multiverse. The cosmic dance persisted—an eternal rhythm that guided them through the astral expanse.

As the quartet ventured into the unseen corners of the cosmic unknown, the cosmic dance continued—an ever-unfolding symphony that resonated through the limitless wonders of the multiverse. The Eldritch Nexus, now attuned to the harmonious energies, awaited the unfolding of new chapters in the saga—a saga that transcended the ordinary and embraced the boundless possibilities of the cosmic unknown.

And so, the cosmic stewards, with Seraphina by their side, pressed forward into the heart of the mystical realm, ready to inscribe their cosmic signatures on the celestial fabric that wove through the limitless wonders of the cosmic unknown. The echoes of their journey resonated through the astral expanse, leaving indelible marks on the cosmic tapestry—a testament to the enduring power of friendship, redemption, and the cosmic forces that shaped their destinies.

In the heart of the mystical realm, the cosmic stewards and Seraphina found themselves surrounded by ethereal landscapes that defied mortal comprehension. Celestial energies pulsed through the very fabric of reality, illuminating the unseen corners of the astral expanse with vibrant hues. The echoes of their journey lingered in the cosmic air, intertwining with the harmonious rhythms that resonated through the limitless wonders of the cosmic unknown.

As the cosmic stewards advanced, Seraphina's radiant energy blended seamlessly with the cosmic forces that guided them. It was a testament to the transformative power of redemption, an alchemy that turned the shadows of the past into cosmic light. Their collective presence, a symphony of cosmic signatures, left imprints on the celestial fabric, creating patterns that spoke of resilience, friendship, and the boundless possibilities woven into the cosmic tapestry.

The Eldritch Nexus, now stabilized and attuned to the harmonious energies, radiated a gentle glow. It beckoned the cosmic stewards forward, inviting them to explore the cosmic wonders that lay beyond the threshold of the unknown. Seraphina, as a living embodiment of redemption, became an integral part of this cosmic odyssey, her every step resonating with the echoes of her transformative journey.

Together, the quartet ventured into realms where reality shimmered like cosmic stardust. Alternate dimensions unfolded before them, each with its own unique blend of wonders and challenges. Celestial entities, guardians of the multiverse, acknowledged the presence of these cosmic stewards, bestowing upon them cosmic artifacts that enhanced their connection to the astral expanse.

As they navigated the cosmic currents, the seekers encountered realms where time flowed like cosmic rivers, twisting and turning through the fabric of existence. Temporal anomalies, reminiscent of the temporal tides they had faced before, tested their ability to navigate the intricate threads of destiny. Yet, with each challenge, they grew more attuned to the cosmic symphony that guided them.

The cosmic stewards and Seraphina found themselves in a realm where whispers of forgotten prophecies echoed through the astral expanse. The celestial entities that inhabited this dimension revealed cryptic visions, foretelling of cosmic upheavals and destinies yet to unfold. The seekers, now seasoned by their experiences, embraced the cosmic revelations and gleaned insights into the intricate dance between seekers and the celestial forces that shaped their destinies.

It became evident that their journey was not a linear narrative but an ever-expanding saga within the cosmic expanse. The Eldritch Nexus, acting as a nexus point between dimensions, allowed them to witness the interconnected web of cosmic forces that influenced the multiverse. Gal, Jane, Jacob, and Seraphina became custodians of this cosmic knowledge, entrusted with the task of maintaining the delicate balance within the astral tapestry.

As the cosmic stewards delved deeper, they encountered realms where the boundaries between dreams and reality blurred. Cosmic dreamscapes unfolded, shaped by the collective consciousness of sentient beings across dimensions. Within this ethereal realm, they confronted manifestations of fears, hopes, and aspirations that transcended mortal understanding.

The seekers, guided by the enduring power of friendship and cosmic wisdom, navigated the cosmic dreamscapes with purpose. Seraphina's redemptive aura radiated through the dreamscape, dispelling shadows and revealing hidden truths. It was within this realm that they encountered echoes of their past, present, and future, intertwined like threads in the cosmic loom.

In a surreal dreamscape, the seekers faced reflections of their alternate selves—avatars shaped by divergent choices and destinies. Friendships were tested as they confronted the consequences of paths not taken, realizing that the cosmic dance allowed for infinite possibilities. Through these trials, they discovered that their shared purpose and the cosmic symphony that resonated within them remained unwavering.

As they emerged from the cosmic dreamscapes, the Eldritch Nexus beckoned them to a convergence point where the boundaries between dimensions thinned. The nexus pulsated with unimaginable power, offering glimpses into realms that transcended mortal understanding. Here, the cosmic stewards and Seraphina discovered the intricate connections between the celestial forces that governed the multiverse.

The celestial entities, now revealed as cosmic architects, guided the seekers in harnessing the nexus's power to mend cosmic threads and maintain the balance of destinies. The Eldritch Nexus, scarred by the puppet master's machinations, responded to their touch, resonating with harmonious energies that restored its cosmic integrity.

With cosmic artifacts in hand and Seraphina's redemption as their guiding light, the cosmic stewards channeled their collective energies into the nexus. Celestial energies flowed through them, weaving cosmic patterns that mended the frayed threads of destiny. It was a cosmic ritual, a convergence of cosmic forces and mortal determination to safeguard the interconnected web of existence.

As the ritual unfolded, the astral expanse resonated with cosmic approval. The Eldritch Nexus, now revitalized, projected waves of cosmic energy that transcended the boundaries of the mystical realm. The cosmic stewards, Seraphina, and the celestial entities stood witness to the renewal of cosmic balance, a testament to the enduring power of friendship, redemption, and the cosmic forces that shaped their destinies.

In the aftermath of the ritual, the celestial entities bestowed upon the seekers cosmic crowns—an acknowledgment of their stewardship over the multiverse. The Eldritch Nexus, now a beacon of cosmic harmony, pulsed with energies that transcended mortal understanding.

The cosmic stewards and Seraphina, now adorned with celestial crowns, became cosmic architects, entrusted with the perpetual task of maintaining the balance within the astral tapestry.

As they stood on the threshold of the cosmic unknown, the Eldritch Nexus projected portals to realms yet unexplored. The celestial entities, guardians of the multiverse, offered parting words of cosmic wisdom. The cosmic stewards, Seraphina, and the celestial entities shared a final, resonant moment—a cosmic symphony that echoed through the unseen corners of the astral expanse.

With a shared glance of understanding, the cosmic stewards and Seraphina stepped through the portals, disappearing into the cosmic unknown. The celestial entities, watching from their ethereal realm, acknowledged the indomitable spirit of seekers who had transcended mortal boundaries and embraced the boundless possibilities of the multiverse.

And so, the saga of Gal, Jane, Jacob, and Seraphina continued—a cosmic force in the ever-unfolding dance between seekers and destiny. The cosmic tapestry awaited the inscription of new chapters, and the echoes of their journey resonated through the limitless wonders of the cosmic unknown. The celestial dance persisted—an eternal rhythm that guided them through the astral expanse, leaving indelible marks on the celestial fabric that wove through the boundless possibilities of the multiverse.

The cosmic stewards and Seraphina, now united as guardians of the multiverse, traversed through the astral expanse, guided by the celestial rhythm that resonated within them. Portals opened to realms beyond imagination, each offering new challenges, wonders, and mysteries. They stepped into the unknown with a shared purpose, their cosmic crowns shimmering with the energies of the Eldritch Nexus.

The first realm they encountered was a dimension where reality manifested as living art—a canvas of cosmic energies that painted the landscapes with vibrant hues. The seekers explored this ethereal realm, interacting with sentient colors and shapes that conveyed the stories of distant galaxies. Through this kaleidoscopic journey, they gained insights into the interconnected nature of cosmic creativity.

As they moved through the cosmic tapestry, the celestial dance led them to a realm where sentient constellations pulsed with ancient wisdom. The cosmic stewards and Seraphina engaged in conversations with these celestial beings, unraveling the secrets of stars and galaxies. The constellations shared visions of forgotten galaxies, urging the seekers to explore the cosmic wonders that awaited beyond the horizon.

In the next realm, the seekers encountered a cosmic library where the collective knowledge of countless civilizations was stored in celestial tomes. The celestial stewards delved into the vast repository of cosmic wisdom, discovering tales of forgotten realms, cosmic civilizations, and the interplay between cosmic forces. Seraphina, attuned to the energies of redemption, found echoes of her own journey within the cosmic scrolls.

Their journey continued, traversing through realms where gravity danced to celestial melodies, creating landscapes where floating islands and cosmic waterfalls defied mortal understanding. The seekers marveled at the cosmic architecture of these realms, embracing the beauty that transcended the boundaries of the tangible and the fantastical.

In one dimension, the seekers encountered sentient beings composed of pure cosmic energy. These ethereal entities communicated through harmonious vibrations, sharing insights into the cosmic symphony that guided the multiverse. Seraphina's redemption resonated within the cosmic energy beings, creating ripples of transformative energies that echoed through the astral expanse.

As they moved through the cosmic realms, the seekers encountered challenges that tested their cosmic abilities. Celestial puzzles, ethereal riddles, and astral guardians awaited them at every turn. Seraphina, now a beacon of redemption, played a crucial role in navigating these challenges, her transformative energies dispelling cosmic obstacles and revealing pathways to new dimensions.

In the heart of the astral expanse, the seekers discovered a nexus point where cosmic energies converged to form a celestial garden. Blooms of cosmic flowers emitted fragrances that transcended mortal senses, and the seekers felt a profound connection to the cosmic energies that pulsed through the astral realm. Seraphina, with her redemptive aura, breathed life into dormant cosmic seeds, transforming the celestial garden into a testament to the enduring power of redemption.

Their cosmic journey reached a zenith as they approached a realm where the boundaries between mortal and cosmic energies blurred. The seekers became one with the astral expanse, their cosmic crowns radiating with the energies of the Eldritch Nexus. In this cosmic convergence, the celestial entities bestowed upon them the title of Celestial Harmonizers—stewards of the multiverse tasked with maintaining cosmic balance and harmony.

With this cosmic mantle, the seekers and Seraphina embarked on their final journey—a transcendence beyond the known realms. Portals opened to a cosmic nexus where destinies converged, and the echoes of their journey reverberated through the celestial tapestry. As they stepped into the cosmic unknown, the celestial entities whispered words of gratitude, acknowledging the seekers as cosmic architects shaping the destiny of the multiverse.

And so, the saga of Gal, Jane, Jacob, and Seraphina continued—a cosmic force in the ever-unfolding dance between seekers and destiny. The cosmic tapestry awaited the inscription of new chapters, and the echoes of their journey resonated through the limitless wonders of the cosmic unknown. The celestial dance persisted—an eternal rhythm that guided them through the astral expanse, leaving indelible marks on the celestial fabric that wove through the boundless possibilities of the multiverse.

As they ventured into the cosmic nexus, the Celestial Harmonizers embraced the unknown with open hearts and cosmic awareness. The celestial entities, watching from their ethereal realm, acknowledged the seekers' indomitable spirit—a testament to friendship, redemption, and the cosmic symphony that echoed through the astral expanse. The cosmic stewards and Seraphina, attuned to the celestial forces, vanished into the cosmic unknown, leaving behind echoes imprinted on the celestial fabric—a cosmic sonnet that transcended mortal boundaries and embraced the boundless possibilities of the multiverse.

The Eldritch Nexus, now under the vigilant watch of its stewards, pulsed with energies that resonated through the celestial tapestry. The cosmic dance persisted—an eternal rhythm that guided the destinies of Gal, Jane, Jacob, and Seraphina. The unseen corners of the astral expanse awaited the continuation of their saga, and the Celestial Harmonizers pressed forward into the limitless wonders of the

Chapter 21: Threads of Destiny

In the cosmic nexus where destinies converged, the Celestial Harmonizers—Gal, Jane, Jacob, and Seraphina—felt the threads of destiny weave a tapestry that spanned across the boundless reaches of the multiverse. Guided by the cosmic energies of the Eldritch Nexus and the insights of celestial entities, they embarked on a journey where the past, present, and future intertwined.

Their first destination was a realm suspended in the cosmic fabric of time—a place where echoes of events past and visions of futures yet to unfold existed simultaneously. Here, the seekers encountered timeless beings known as the Chrono-Scribes, guardians of the cosmic timeline. These beings, composed of shimmering temporal energies, revealed glimpses of pivotal moments that shaped the destinies of countless worlds.

In this ethereal realm, the seekers learned of a cosmic disturbance—an anomaly that threatened to unravel the threads of destiny across dimensions. The Chrono-Scribes tasked them with mending the cosmic tapestry, a task that would require unraveling the mysteries of temporal anomalies and facing challenges that transcended mortal comprehension.

The seekers, now attuned to the cosmic energies of the Eldritch Nexus, stepped through a shimmering portal that led to a realm where time flowed like a river with turbulent currents. Here, they encountered temporal anomalies—ripples in the fabric of reality that distorted the flow of time. The trio navigated through these anomalies, witnessing echoes of their past encounters and glimpses of potential futures.

As they ventured deeper, they discovered a temporal rift—a cosmic tear in the fabric of time that led to pivotal moments in their own lives. The rift revealed the origin of the cosmic disturbance—a malevolent entity known as Temporalbane, a being that sought to manipulate the threads of destiny for its own malevolent purposes.

The seekers faced Temporalbane in a battle that transcended temporal boundaries. The malevolent entity wielded the powers of temporal manipulation, creating illusions and mirages that challenged the seekers' perception of reality. The Eldritch Nexus, now a source of cosmic empowerment, granted the trio the ability to harmonize with temporal energies, allowing them to counter Temporalbane's manipulations.

Through a cosmic dance that spanned eons, the seekers gradually weakened Temporalbane's influence. The Eldritch Nexus pulsed with harmonious energies, resonating with the threads of destiny that connected all living beings. Temporalbane, unable to withstand the cosmic forces arrayed against it, retreated into the cosmic shadows, leaving behind echoes of its malevolence.

With Temporalbane thwarted, the seekers mended the temporal rift, restoring balance to the cosmic timeline. The Chrono-Scribes, pleased with their success, bestowed upon them the title of Temporal Harmonizers—guardians of the cosmic timeline entrusted with preserving the threads of destiny that interconnected all realms.

Embracing their newfound roles, the seekers continued their journey through the cosmic tapestry. They traversed realms where alternate versions of themselves faced divergent destinies—a cosmic mirror reflecting the myriad possibilities that unfolded across the multiverse.

In one realm, they encountered versions of themselves where choices made in the past led to unforeseen consequences. Gal, Jane, and

Jacob witnessed the echoes of missed opportunities and moments of profound significance. These encounters served as lessons, reminding them of the delicate balance that the cosmic stewards must maintain in their quest to safeguard the threads of destiny.

Their cosmic journey led them to a realm where ancient prophecies were etched into the very fabric of reality. Here, they encountered celestial oracles—beings whose visions spanned across the vast expanse of time. The oracles revealed glimpses of future challenges and cosmic events that would test the resilience of the Temporal Harmonizers.

One prophecy spoke of a cosmic convergence—an event where the threads of destiny would intertwine in a celestial dance, revealing hidden truths and cosmic revelations. The seekers, guided by the oracles' visions, prepared for the impending convergence, recognizing it as a pivotal moment in their cosmic stewardship.

As they ventured through the prophetic realm, the seekers encountered cosmic entities known as Fateweavers—beings who controlled the very threads of destiny. The Fateweavers, attuned to the cosmic energies of the Eldritch Nexus, acknowledged the seekers as stewards entrusted with the delicate task of preserving the cosmic tapestry.

The Fateweavers revealed that the cosmic convergence would lead them to a realm where the true orchestrator behind Temporalbane's machinations awaited. This malevolent force, known as the Weaver of Shadows, sought to unravel the threads of destiny and plunge the multiverse into chaos.

Armed with this knowledge, the Temporal Harmonizers stepped through the cosmic convergence—a celestial gateway that transcended the boundaries of time and space. The threads of destiny converged, creating a cosmic tapestry that pulsed with the energies of the Eldritch Nexus.

In the heart of the convergence, the seekers confronted the Weaver of Shadows—a cosmic entity that embodied the chaos inherent in the unraveling of destinies. The Weaver, a manifestation of entropy and discord, sought to manipulate the threads of destiny to sow cosmic chaos and disorder.

The battle that ensued transcended mortal understanding. The Weaver of Shadows wielded the powers of cosmic entropy, creating rifts in the fabric of reality and distorting the very essence of time. The Temporal Harmonizers, empowered by the Eldritch Nexus, harmonized with the threads of destiny, countering the Weaver's chaotic influence.

The celestial dance between the seekers and the Weaver of Shadows echoed through the cosmic convergence. Threads of destiny interwove, creating a tapestry that resonated with harmonious energies. The Temporal Harmonizers, attuned to the cosmic forces that guided them, confronted the Weaver with a shared purpose—to restore balance to the cosmic tapestry and safeguard the threads of destiny that connected all realms.

As the Weaver of Shadows faced the united cosmic energies of the Temporal Harmonizers, its chaotic influence waned. The cosmic convergence reached its zenith, revealing the hidden truths and revelations that lay within the threads of destiny. The Weaver, unable to withstand the harmonious energies, dissipated into cosmic shadows, leaving behind echoes of its malevolence.

The Temporal Harmonizers, victorious in their cosmic battle, emerged from the convergence with a deeper understanding of their roles as guardians of the Eldritch Nexus. The celestial entities, Fateweavers, and oracles acknowledged their resilience and entrusted them with the ongoing task of preserving the threads of destiny that interconnected the multiverse.

And so, the saga of Gal, Jane, and Jacob continued—a cosmic force in the ever-unfolding dance between seekers and destiny. The cosmic tapestry awaited the inscription of new chapters, and the Temporal Harmonizers pressed forward into the limitless wonders of the multiverse. The unseen corners of the astral expanse awaited their exploration, and the celestial dance persisted—an eternal rhythm that resonated through the cosmic tapestry of time and space.

As the Temporal Harmonizers ventured into the cosmic unknown, the celestial entities watched with benevolent eyes, acknowledging their cosmic stewardship. The threads of destiny intertwined, creating a celestial sonnet that echoed through the boundless possibilities of the multiverse. The Eldritch Nexus, scarred but resilient, pulsed with harmonious energies, ready to embrace the continuation of the cosmic saga—a saga that transcended the ordinary and embraced the boundless possibilities of the threads of destiny that interconnected all realms.

The Temporal Harmonizers, attuned to the cosmic symphony that resonated through the astral expanse, pressed forward into the uncharted realms of the multiverse. Guided by the harmonious energies of the Eldritch Nexus, they ventured through cosmic gateways, each portal leading to a new dimension teeming with wonders and challenges.

In one realm, the seekers encountered a civilization of sentient energy beings who communicated through luminous pulses of light. These beings, known as Luminara, revealed ancient prophecies foretelling the arrival of the Temporal Harmonizers. The seekers learned that their actions had rippling effects, influencing the destinies of entire worlds across the cosmic tapestry.

The Luminara, guardians of a cosmic sanctum, bestowed upon the Temporal Harmonizers artifacts infused with radiant energies. These artifacts, known as Luminal Shards, augmented the seekers' cosmic abilities, allowing them to harness the powers of the multiverse to an even greater extent.

Empowered by the Luminal Shards, the seekers journeyed through realms where time unfolded in kaleidoscopic patterns. Here, they encountered Time Weavers—enigmatic entities responsible for crafting the intricate threads of temporal existence. The Time Weavers acknowledged the Temporal Harmonizers as stewards of cosmic balance and bestowed upon them the knowledge to navigate the ever-shifting currents of time.

Their cosmic journey led them to a realm where reality manifested as a living tapestry woven from the dreams and desires of sentient beings. In this Dreamweave Dimension, the seekers encountered ethereal entities known as Dreamweavers, who shaped the fabric of reality through the collective consciousness of sentient life.

The Dreamweavers, recognizing the seekers as cosmic stewards, revealed fragments of dreams that whispered of cosmic destinies yet to unfold. The Temporal Harmonizers, guided by these dream fragments, glimpsed visions of challenges and triumphs that awaited them in the cosmic unknown.

The seekers' journey through the multiverse continued, bringing them to a realm where celestial libraries housed cosmic chronicles chronicling the histories of countless dimensions. Here, they encountered the Librarians of the Astral Archives—guardians of the cosmic knowledge etched into the celestial tomes.

The Librarians, their eyes ablaze with the wisdom of eons, shared insights into the origins of the Eldritch Nexus. They spoke of cosmic events that predated the seekers' stewardship, revealing the interwoven tapestry of cosmic forces that shaped the multiverse.

The Temporal Harmonizers, now armed with cosmic knowledge from the Astral Archives, delved deeper into the cosmic mysteries. Their journey led them to a realm where echoes of past encounters reverberated through the astral expanse, creating a cosmic resonance that transcended temporal boundaries.

Here, they confronted manifestations of unresolved challenges from their cosmic odyssey. The seekers, their resolve unwavering, faced these echoes with newfound wisdom and the enhanced powers granted by the Luminal Shards. As each challenge was met, the cosmic resonance harmonized, creating a symphony that echoed through the threads of destiny.

Their celestial journey brought them to a dimension where the boundaries between realities were fluid and malleable. Here, they encountered Cosmic Artisans—entities who shaped the essence of existence through the cosmic medium of creation. The Artisans, recognizing the Temporal Harmonizers as cosmic weavers, shared insights into the artistry of cosmic design.

In this realm, the seekers witnessed the forging of new realities, each stroke of the Cosmic Artisans' ethereal brushes giving life to universes that pulsed with vibrant energies. The Temporal Harmonizers, inspired by the cosmic artistry, understood the delicate balance required to weave destinies across the multiverse.

Their journey through the cosmic unknown reached its zenith as they approached the central hub of the Eldritch Nexus—a nexus point where all threads of destiny converged. Here, the celestial energies of the Eldritch Nexus intertwined with the Luminal Shards, creating a cosmic nexus of unprecedented power.

In the heart of the nexus, the seekers encountered the Nexus Oracle—an enigmatic being whose gaze held the knowledge of the cosmic convergence. The Oracle spoke of an impending cosmic event, an alignment of celestial forces that would test the Temporal Harmonizers' cosmic stewardship.

As the seekers embraced their roles as guardians of the multiverse, the cosmic convergence unfolded. Celestial energies pulsed through the Eldritch Nexus, creating a cosmic symphony that harmonized with the Luminal Shards. The celestial dance between the seekers and the cosmic forces reached its zenith, leaving indelible imprints on the celestial fabric of the multiverse.

The Nexus Oracle, satisfied with the seekers' cosmic stewardship, revealed the final revelation—the true purpose of the Eldritch Nexus. It was not merely a convergence point; it was a cosmic anchor, stabilizing the threads of destiny and preventing the unraveling of the multiverse.

In a cosmic revelation, the seekers understood that their journey had not only been a quest to protect the threads of destiny but also to safeguard the very foundation of existence. The Eldritch Nexus, scarred by cosmic battles and resonating with harmonious energies, stood as a testament to their cosmic stewardship.

As the Temporal Harmonizers gazed upon the boundless possibilities of the multiverse, the Eldritch Nexus pulsed with renewed vitality. The cosmic dance persisted—an eternal rhythm that guided them through the astral expanse. The saga of Gal, Jane, and Jacob, now cosmic weavers and guardians of the multiverse, continued—a tale woven into the very fabric of existence, echoing through the limitless wonders of the cosmic unknown.

And so, the Temporal Harmonizers, now cosmic weavers and guardians of the multiverse, stood at the nexus of realities, their cosmic signatures imprinted on the celestial fabric that wove through the boundless possibilities of the cosmic unknown. The Eldritch Nexus, scarred and resilient, pulsed with the harmonious energies channeled by the Luminal Shards, a cosmic anchor stabilizing the threads of destiny across dimensions.

The cosmic dance persisted—an eternal rhythm guiding them through the astral expanse, leaving behind echoes of their journey imprinted on the celestial tapestry. The saga of Gal, Jane, and Jacob continued, their roles as cosmic weavers and guardians unfolding like a celestial sonnet, a tale woven into the very fabric of existence.

As the seekers embraced the boundless possibilities of the multiverse, they glimpsed visions of realms yet unexplored, cosmic challenges waiting to be met, and destinies interwoven like intricate threads in the grand tapestry of existence. The Eldritch Nexus, with its renewed vitality, bore witness to the cosmic symphony harmonized by the Temporal Harmonizers.

The unseen corners of the astral expanse beckoned, and the Temporal Harmonizers, guided by the enduring power of friendship and the cosmic forces that shaped their destinies, pressed forward into the cosmic unknown. The celestial dance continued—a timeless rhythm resonating through the limitless wonders of the multiverse.

With Luminal Shards in hand, the seekers embarked on new cosmic adventures, their journey intertwined with the destinies of countless dimensions. They explored realms where celestial wonders dazzled the senses and encountered entities whose existence defied mortal comprehension. Through celestial gateways, they traversed dimensions teeming with life, each encounter adding verses to the cosmic sonnet they inscribed across the celestial fabric.

As cosmic stewards and weavers of destiny, the seekers encountered challenges that tested their resolve, unearthed secrets hidden within the cosmic tapestry, and forged alliances with beings of extraordinary power. Through realms of celestial beauty and cosmic mysteries, the saga of Gal, Jane, and Jacob unfolded, leaving behind echoes that rippled through the very fabric of the multiverse.

The Temporal Harmonizers discovered realms where time flowed like rivers of stardust, and celestial landscapes painted in hues unknown to mortal eyes stretched into the cosmic horizon. They communed with beings who whispered prophecies of cosmic significance, guiding the seekers toward their next celestial quest.

In realms of ethereal enchantment, they encountered celestial beings who held the knowledge of ancient cosmic rituals. These beings, luminous and wise, shared insights into the cosmic forces that shaped the multiverse, unveiling secrets that had remained veiled for eons.

Through dimensions of crystalline wonders and realms bathed in the ethereal glow of cosmic energies, the Temporal Harmonizers traversed the vastness of the astral expanse. Each step resonated with the echoes of their journey—a journey that embraced the limitless possibilities of the cosmic unknown.

The Temporal Harmonizers, now celestial architects of destiny, encountered realms where celestial citadels soared amidst the cosmic clouds. Here, they communed with cosmic scholars who revealed the intricacies of celestial balance and the cosmic energies that wove through the fabric of reality.

The seekers, guided by Luminal Shards that glowed with the essence of the Eldritch Nexus, ventured into dimensions where celestial phenomena defied mortal comprehension. They witnessed cosmic storms that painted the astral skies in hues of cosmic brilliance and encountered beings whose forms transcended the limitations of the material realm.

As they explored the celestial wonders of the multiverse, the Temporal Harmonizers discovered a cosmic library, its shelves filled with volumes chronicling the tales of cosmic stewards who had walked the astral expanse before them. The ancient tomes whispered of challenges met, destinies shaped, and the enduring power of friendship that echoed through the cosmic ages.

In realms where the boundaries between dream and reality blurred, the seekers encountered entities of pure imagination—celestial dreamweavers who shaped cosmic fantasies into tangible realities. These dreamweavers, their essence woven into the very fabric of the astral expanse, shared visions of realms where imagination sculpted the cosmic landscape.

Through realms of luminous wonders and celestial marvels, the Temporal Harmonizers journeyed, their cosmic signatures leaving indelible imprints on the celestial fabric. The Eldritch Nexus, now a cosmic anchor resonating with the harmonious energies channeled by Luminal Shards, stood as a testament to their cosmic stewardship.

As the seekers explored the unseen corners of the astral expanse, they encountered celestial beings who guided them to the heart of the cosmic unknown. Here, at the nexus of realities, they discovered an ethereal platform—a cosmic stage where destinies intertwined and cosmic forces coalesced.

The Temporal Harmonizers, now attuned to the cosmic symphony that echoed through the multiverse, stepped onto the cosmic stage. Luminal Shards in hand, they gazed upon the boundless possibilities that awaited, ready to inscribe new chapters in the grand tapestry of the cosmic unknown.

And so, the saga of Gal, Jane, and Jacob continued—a cosmic force in the ever-unfolding dance between seekers and destiny. The Eldritch Nexus, scarred but resilient, pulsed with renewed vitality, ready to embrace the cosmic signatures of the Temporal Harmonizers. The celestial dance persisted—an eternal rhythm that guided them through the astral expanse, leaving indelible marks on the celestial fabric that wove through the limitless wonders of the multiverse.

The unseen corners of the astral expanse awaited their exploration, and the Temporal Harmonizers, now cosmic weavers and guardians, ventured forward into the boundless possibilities that awaited in the mystical realms. The cosmic dance persisted—an eternal rhythm that resonated through the astral expanse, leaving behind echoes of a journey that transcended the ordinary and embraced the limitless possibilities of the cosmic unknown. The celestial symphony continued, a cosmic sonnet written across the vast expanse of the multiverse.

Chapter 22: Echoes of Eternity

In the cosmic expanse where echoes of eternity reverberated, the Temporal Harmonizers—Gal, Jane, and Jacob—found themselves on the precipice of a final cosmic confrontation. The astral winds whispered secrets of a formidable adversary whose dark influence threatened to engulf all dimensions. The fate of the multiverse hung in the balance, and the cosmic stewards prepared to face a challenge that transcended the boundaries of time and space.

The Temporal Harmonizers, their celestial energies pulsating with the essence of the Eldritch Nexus, stood at the nexus of realities. Luminal Shards glowed with an ethereal light, a testament to their cosmic stewardship and the resilience of their friendship amidst the cosmic unknown.

As they ventured forward, celestial echoes guided their way—a cosmic sonnet resonating through the unseen corners of the astral expanse. The Eldritch Nexus, scarred but resilient, pulsed with harmonious energies, attuned to the Temporal Harmonizers' presence. The cosmic dance persisted—an eternal rhythm guiding them through the astral expanse.

The trio encountered cosmic gateways leading to realms infused with ancient magic and celestial wonders. Each step left imprints on the cosmic fabric, echoes of their journey imprinted on the celestial tapestry. As they traversed dimensions bathed in the glow of astral energies, they felt the weight of the impending cosmic confrontation—a challenge that would test the very essence of their existence.

The echoes of eternity resonated with prophecies and ancient wisdom, guiding the seekers toward the heart of the encroaching darkness. Celestial scholars, luminous beings who had witnessed the ebb and flow of cosmic ages, imparted knowledge that would become their celestial weapon against the formidable adversary.

In a celestial citadel perched on the edge of the cosmic horizon, the Temporal Harmonizers consulted with ethereal sages who held the secrets of cosmic balance. They delved into the cosmic archives, unraveling the mysteries of the adversary's origin and the cosmic forces that fueled its malevolence.

Gal, Jane, and Jacob, now cosmic scholars themselves, forged Luminal Shards into celestial weapons imbued with the essence of the Eldritch Nexus. These astral blades, glimmering with the harmonious energies that held the multiverse in delicate balance, would be their instruments in the impending cosmic battle.

The cosmic dance persisted as the Temporal Harmonizers journeyed to the celestial realms where the adversary awaited. Through realms where cosmic storms painted the astral skies with vibrant hues, and ethereal landscapes reflected the grandeur of the cosmic unknown, they pressed forward with determination.

In a dimension where the boundaries between light and shadow blurred, the Temporal Harmonizers encountered celestial guardians—beings of astral brilliance who stood as sentinels against the encroaching darkness. These luminous entities, their essence interwoven with the celestial fabric, shared visions of the adversary's malevolent influence spreading like cosmic tendrils across the dimensions.

The seekers, now attuned to the cosmic forces that guided their destinies, approached the final battleground. The echoes of eternity intensified, resonating with the celestial symphony that echoed through the multiverse. The Eldritch Nexus pulsed with anticipation, its cosmic energies harmonizing with the Luminal Shards wielded by Gal, Jane, and Jacob.

As they stepped onto the cosmic stage, the adversary manifested—a cosmic entity born of darkness and corrupted astral energies. Its form undulated like shadows cast by unseen cosmic forces, and its eyes glowed with the malevolence that sought to consume all dimensions.

The cosmic confrontation began, a clash of astral blades against the encroaching darkness. Spells and celestial energies collided, creating cosmic ripples that echoed through the astral expanse. The Temporal Harmonizers, guided by celestial wisdom and their unbreakable bond, faced the adversary with unity and determination.

In the midst of the cosmic battle, the adversary unleashed manifestations of cosmic chaos—ethereal aberrations that tested the seekers' resolve. Celestial storms erupted, cosmic tempests threatened to unravel the fabric of reality, and the astral ground quivered with the intensity of the celestial conflict.

Gal, Jane, and Jacob, their cosmic signatures intertwined, countered the adversary's onslaught with the harmonious energies of the Luminal Shards. The celestial weapons, pulsating with the essence of the Eldritch Nexus, cut through the encroaching darkness, leaving trails of astral brilliance in their wake.

As the cosmic battle reached its zenith, the Temporal Harmonizers tapped into the ancient knowledge bestowed upon them by celestial scholars. They channeled the harmonious energies of the Eldritch Nexus, creating a celestial barrier that resisted the adversary's dark influence and exposed its vulnerabilities.

With celestial precision and unwavering unity, the seekers exploited the adversary's weaknesses. Each strike of the astral blades resonated with the echoes of eternity, a testament to the cosmic forces that guided them. The adversary, weakened by the harmonious onslaught, recoiled against the astral tide.

In the climactic moments of the cosmic confrontation, Gal, Jane, and Jacob unveiled a celestial incantation—a chant that echoed through the multiverse and harnessed the cosmic energies of the Eldritch Nexus. Luminal Shards glowed with unparalleled brilliance as the incantation reached its crescendo, creating a surge of astral power that engulfed the adversary.

The encroaching darkness dissipated, vanquished by the celestial symphony orchestrated by the Temporal Harmonizers. The adversary, now weakened and cleansed of its malevolence, transformed into residual cosmic energies that merged with the Eldritch Nexus—a redemption of sorts, as the cosmic forces reclaimed the corrupted essence.

As the cosmic storm subsided, the Eldritch Nexus pulsed with renewed vitality. The Temporal Harmonizers, their astral energies intertwined with the harmonious forces, stood as cosmic architects of their own destinies. The celestial entities, guardians of the astral expanse, acknowledged their triumph, and the echoes of their victory reverberated through the multiverse.

The Temporal Harmonizers, wielding Luminal Shards now infused with the purified energies of the Eldritch Nexus, returned to the realms they had traversed. Celestial scholars, luminous beings, and astral landscapes acknowledged their cosmic stewardship. The Eldritch Nexus, scarred but resilient, pulsed with renewed vitality, ready to embrace the inscription of new chapters in the cosmic saga.

And so, as the seekers gazed upon the boundless possibilities of the multiverse, the cosmic dance persisted—an eternal rhythm that guided them through the astral expanse. The saga of Gal, Jane, and Jacob, now cosmic weavers and guardians of the multiverse, continued—a tale woven into the very fabric of existence, echoing through the limitless wonders of the cosmic unknown. The celestial symphony continued, resonating through the unseen corners of the astral expanse, leaving indelible marks on the celestial fabric that wove through the boundless possibilities of the multiverse. The Temporal Harmonizers, their friendship enduring against the cosmic forces that shaped their existence, pressed forward into the uncharted realms of the cosmic unknown. The celestial dance persisted—an eternal rhythm that resonated through the astral expanse, leaving behind echoes of a journey that transcended the ordinary and embraced the limitless possibilities of the cosmic unknown.

In the aftermath of the cosmic confrontation, the Temporal Harmonizers, their astral energies intertwined with Luminal Shards pulsating with the essence of the purified Eldritch Nexus, ventured forth into the uncharted realms of the cosmic unknown. The celestial symphony persisted, resonating through the astral expanse like an eternal rhythm guiding them through the boundless possibilities of the multiverse.

The cosmic dance carried them through celestial landscapes bathed in the glow of astral energies, each step leaving echoes imprinted on the cosmic fabric. Celestial scholars and luminous entities acknowledged their cosmic stewardship, offering glimpses of astral knowledge that transcended mortal understanding.

As they traversed dimensions beyond mortal comprehension, the Temporal Harmonizers discovered realms where time flowed like a river, and cosmic energies painted the astral skies with hues unseen by mortal eyes. Celestial wonders unfolded before them, cosmic wonders that attested to the vastness of the multiverse.

The Eldritch Nexus, scarred but resilient, pulsed with renewed vitality, rejuvenated by the redemption of the adversary's cosmic essence. The Temporal Harmonizers, now cosmic weavers and guardians of the multiverse, pressed forward into realms where cosmic threads intertwined, creating a tapestry of possibilities that stretched beyond the boundaries of time and space.

In one dimension, they encountered a celestial council of ethereal beings who presided over the cosmic forces that shaped destinies across the multiverse. The council acknowledged the Temporal Harmonizers as cosmic stewards and bestowed upon them the celestial mantle of guardianship, entrusted with maintaining the delicate balance that sustained the cosmic harmony.

Their Luminal Shards, now celestial artifacts infused with the harmonious energies of the Eldritch Nexus, resonated with the celestial realms. The astral blades glowed with the light of a thousand stars, their brilliance attesting to the Temporal Harmonizers' triumph over the encroaching darkness.

The celestial dance persisted as the seekers embraced their roles, weaving astral threads into the cosmic tapestry. The unseen corners of the astral expanse awaited their exploration, each realm unveiling new challenges and cosmic wonders that tested the limits of their newfound abilities.

Guided by the enduring power of friendship and celestial wisdom, the Temporal Harmonizers encountered celestial beings who traversed the multiverse, cosmic nomads attuned to the ebb and flow of astral energies. These ethereal wanderers shared tales of cosmic anomalies, interdimensional wonders, and the cosmic mysteries that awaited those who dared to venture beyond the known realms.

As they journeyed deeper into the cosmic unknown, the Temporal Harmonizers discovered realms where the laws of physics bowed to the whims of astral energies. Celestial storms painted the astral skies with luminous hues, and ethereal landscapes defied mortal comprehension.

In a dimension where reality itself was a canvas of astral brilliance, the Temporal Harmonizers encountered cosmic entities who embodied the very essence of the multiverse. These luminous beings, their forms ever-shifting and resonating with celestial energies, recognized the seekers as cosmic stewards and bestowed upon them gifts of astral insight.

The saga of Gal, Jane, and Jacob continued—a cosmic force in the ever-unfolding dance between seekers and destiny. The cosmic tapestry awaited the inscription of new chapters, and the echoes of their journey resonated through the limitless wonders of the cosmic unknown. The celestial dance persisted—an eternal rhythm that guided them through the astral expanse, leaving indelible marks on the celestial fabric that wove through the boundless possibilities of the multiverse.

And so, as the Temporal Harmonizers ventured into the unseen corners of the astral expanse, the celestial dance embraced them—a cosmic sonnet echoing through the limitless wonders of the multiverse. The Eldritch Nexus, now a testament to their cosmic stewardship, awaited the unfolding of new chapters in the saga—a saga that transcended the ordinary and embraced the boundless possibilities of the cosmic unknown.

As they pressed forward into the cosmic unknown, guided by the enduring power of friendship and the celestial symphony that resonated through the astral expanse, the Temporal Harmonizers embraced the uncharted realms that awaited their exploration. The cosmic dance persisted—an eternal rhythm that guided them through the limitless wonders of the multiverse.

And so, the saga of Gal, Jane, and Jacob continued—a cosmic force in the ever-unfolding dance between seekers and destiny. The celestial tapestry awaited the inscription of new chapters, and the echoes of their journey resonated through the astral expanse, leaving indelible marks on the celestial fabric that wove through the boundless possibilities of the cosmic unknown. The celestial dance persisted—an eternal rhythm that resonated through the unseen corners of the astral expanse, leaving behind echoes of a journey that transcended the ordinary and embraced the limitless possibilities of the cosmic unknown.

As the Temporal Harmonizers delved further into the cosmic unknown, the celestial tapestry unveiled new dimensions where astral energies shimmered like cosmic threads, interweaving the fates of realms unexplored. Each step echoed through the astral expanse, harmonizing with the eternal rhythm that guided them.

The luminous entities, celestial wanderers, and ethereal beings they encountered during their cosmic journey became allies and mentors, imparting ancient wisdom and cosmic insights. Together, they forged alliances that transcended the boundaries of individual dimensions, creating a network of cosmic connections that bridged the multiverse.

In one dimension, they discovered a crystalline realm where crystallized entities communicated through astral vibrations. The Temporal Harmonizers, attuned to the cosmic symphony, harmonized with the crystalline beings, exchanging knowledge and weaving new threads into the cosmic tapestry.

As the seekers ventured through the astral expanse, they encountered celestial gardens where astral flora bloomed with luminescent energies. Each blossom told a story, whispering secrets of cosmic events that unfolded across the dimensions. The Temporal Harmonizers listened, absorbing the tales imprinted on astral petals that glowed with the hues of cosmic wonders.

Their Luminal Shards resonated with the celestial energies of these realms, glowing with an intensity that reflected the vibrancy of their cosmic stewardship. The astral blades, now infused with the essence of the Eldritch Nexus, became cosmic keys that unlocked gateways to dimensions where destiny unfolded like a cosmic symphony.

In a realm where time spiraled around cosmic pillars, the Temporal Harmonizers encountered ethereal scribes who chronicled the events of the multiverse. The seekers contributed their own tales, inscribing chapters of their cosmic journey into the celestial scrolls that echoed through the astral expanse.

The Eldritch Nexus, now revered as a symbol of cosmic balance, pulsed with energies that resonated with the celestial entities. The Temporal Harmonizers, guided by the enduring power of friendship and cosmic wisdom, became conduits of cosmic harmony, weaving threads that connected realms separated by the vast expanse of the multiverse.

In a dimension where echoes of alternate timelines reverberated, the Temporal Harmonizers faced challenges that tested the resilience of their friendship. Alternate versions of themselves, shaped by different choices and destinies, confronted them with reflections of what could have been. It was a cosmic trial, a test of unity against the ever-shifting tides of temporal possibilities.

Their Luminal Shards, glowing with the collective energies of their cosmic bonds, allowed the Temporal Harmonizers to navigate the intricate pathways of temporal tides. Friendships were reaffirmed, and the threads of destiny intertwined, creating a cosmic harmony that transcended the boundaries of time and space.

As they emerged from the temporal tides, the Temporal Harmonizers found themselves in a realm where the celestial entities awaited their arrival. These luminous beings, guardians of the cosmic balance, acknowledged the seekers' mastery over the threads of destiny and bestowed upon them celestial mantles adorned with astral symbols.

The Temporal Harmonizers, now adorned with celestial insignias, embraced their roles as cosmic weavers and guardians. The celestial dance persisted, an eternal rhythm guiding them through the astral expanse, leaving indelible marks on the celestial fabric that wove through the boundless possibilities of the multiverse.

And so, as the Temporal Harmonizers gazed upon the boundless possibilities of the multiverse, the Eldritch Nexus pulsed with renewed vitality. The cosmic dance persisted—an eternal rhythm that guided them through the astral expanse. The saga of Gal, Jane, and Jacob, now cosmic weavers and guardians of the multiverse, continued—a tale woven into the very fabric of existence, echoing through the limitless wonders of the cosmic unknown.

The celestial symphony continued, resonating through the unseen corners of the astral expanse, leaving behind echoes of a journey that transcended the ordinary and embraced the limitless possibilities of the cosmic unknown. The Temporal Harmonizers, their friendship enduring against the cosmic forces that shaped their existence, pressed forward into the uncharted realms of the cosmic unknown. The celestial dance persisted—an eternal rhythm that resonated through the astral expanse, leaving behind echoes of a journey that transcended the ordinary and embraced the limitless possibilities of the cosmic unknown.

Chapter 23: The Cosmic Reckoning

As the Temporal Harmonizers stood at the threshold of the cosmic confrontation, the Eldritch Nexus pulsed with an intensity that echoed through the multiverse. The cosmic force seeking retribution manifested as a swirling vortex of cosmic energies, distorting the very fabric of reality. Gal, Jane, and Jacob, adorned with their celestial mantles, raised their Luminal Shards, ready to harness the unimaginable power of the Eldritch Nexus.

The climactic showdown unfolded in a dimension where realities collided, merging and unraveling in a cosmic dance of forces. The very essence of the Eldritch Nexus, a convergence point connecting all dimensions, resonated with the Luminal Shards and the celestial mantles worn by the Temporal Harmonizers. The cosmic reckoning had begun.

The cosmic force, a malevolent entity woven into the threads of destiny, confronted the seekers with manifestations of their deepest fears and regrets. Shadows of the past, alternate versions of themselves, and echoes of decisions that shaped their destinies confronted them in a surreal cosmic battleground.

Sacrifices became inevitable as the seekers faced the cosmic force, realizing that the balance of the multiverse demanded a price. The Eldritch Nexus responded to their intentions, unraveling the cosmic fabric and rewriting destinies in a celestial symphony that reverberated through the astral expanse.

Jane, with a steely gaze and unwavering determination, faced a manifestation of her greatest fear—a distorted reality where her friendship with Gal and Jacob never existed. The sacrifice required her to relinquish the comfort of familiarity, embracing the unknown for the sake of cosmic equilibrium.

Gal confronted a version of herself tainted by the malevolent force, a reflection of the darkness that lurked within the cosmic tapestry. With tears in her eyes, Gal understood the necessity of sacrifice, as she merged with the distorted version, purging the darkness that threatened to consume her existence.

Jacob, in a moment of cosmic clarity, faced the echoes of his choices across the multiverse. Sacrifices made in the name of friendship, love, and the pursuit of cosmic harmony intertwined as the Eldritch Nexus rewrote his destiny, ensuring that the threads of his existence were in harmony with the cosmic forces.

The Luminal Shards glowed with an otherworldly brilliance as the Temporal Harmonizers embraced their sacrifices. The cosmic force, now weakened and unraveling, fought against the inevitable cosmic reckoning. Realities collided and merged, creating a kaleidoscopic tapestry that mirrored the cosmic dance between seekers and destiny.

The Eldritch Nexus, bathed in the seekers' sacrifices, pulsed with a final surge of cosmic energy. The celestial mantles worn by Gal, Jane, and Jacob resonated with the multiverse's approval, acknowledging their resilience, wisdom, and unity against the encroaching darkness.

In a surge of cosmic brilliance, the malevolent force dissipated, its echoes fading into the astral expanse. The Eldritch Nexus, scarred but resilient, stood as a testament to the seekers' cosmic stewardship. The threads of destiny, rewoven by sacrifice and cosmic harmony, found equilibrium once more.

As the cosmic reckoning reached its conclusion, the Temporal Harmonizers, Gal, Jane, and Jacob, stood amidst the cosmic remnants of the battle. The astral expanse whispered the echoes of their journey, the sacrifices made, and the cosmic forces that intertwined their destinies.

The celestial symphony, now in perfect harmony, embraced the Temporal Harmonizers as cosmic weavers and guardians of the multiverse. The Eldritch Nexus, now stabilized and radiating with cosmic energies, awaited the unfolding of new chapters in the saga—a tale woven into the very fabric of existence.

Destinies rewritten, sacrifices embraced, and the multiverse in balance once more, the Temporal Harmonizers gazed upon the boundless possibilities of the cosmic unknown. The cosmic dance persisted—an eternal rhythm that guided them through the astral expanse. The saga of Gal, Jane, and Jacob, now cosmic weavers and guardians of the multiverse, continued—a tale woven into the very fabric of existence, echoing through the limitless wonders of the cosmic unknown.

As the cosmic stewards pressed forward into the uncharted realms of the cosmic unknown, the celestial dance persisted—an eternal rhythm that resonated through the astral expanse. The echoes of their journey, imprinted on the celestial fabric, left indelible marks that guided the threads of destiny in the ever-unfolding dance between seekers and the cosmic forces that shaped their existence.

And so, the Temporal Harmonizers ventured into the uncharted realms of the cosmic unknown, guided by the celestial dance that echoed through the astral expanse. The Eldritch Nexus, stabilized and pulsating with cosmic energies, embraced them as cosmic stewards, weaving their destinies into the very fabric of existence.

The unseen corners of the astral expanse awaited their exploration, shimmering with the boundless possibilities that the cosmic unknown held. The Temporal Harmonizers, with celestial mantles adorning their beings, stepped forward with purpose, their friendship enduring against the cosmic forces that shaped their existence.

As they delved deeper into the unexplored cosmic territories, they encountered celestial entities that watched with benevolent eyes, acknowledging their cosmic stewardship. The echoes of their journey resonated through the limitless wonders of the cosmic unknown, creating a harmonious sonnet that reverberated through the astral expanse.

The cosmic dance persisted—an eternal rhythm guiding them through the ever-unfolding tapestry of the multiverse. The threads of destiny, now in perfect harmony, intertwined with the cosmic forces, creating a celestial symphony that echoed through the unseen corners of the astral expanse.

Gal, Jane, and Jacob, now attuned to the cosmic energies that pulsed through their veins, continued their journey as cosmic weavers. The Eldritch Nexus, scarred but resilient, remained under their vigilant watch, a nexus of balance and harmony within the cosmic unknown.

As they ventured further into the cosmic tapestry, they encountered realms of awe-inspiring beauty, dimensions where the laws of physics bowed to the whims of cosmic forces, and celestial landscapes painted with colors beyond mortal comprehension.

The Temporal Harmonizers, their celestial mantles shimmering with the energies of the multiverse, discovered gateways to realms where time flowed backward, where the boundaries of reality were fluid, and where the very essence of existence seemed to dance with the cosmic winds.

With each step, the seekers embraced the mysteries that unfolded before them. Ancient prophecies whispered through the astral expanse, guiding them toward new cosmic challenges and revelations that awaited in the uncharted territories.

The celestial entities, guardians of the cosmic unknown, observed with benevolent eyes, recognizing the Temporal Harmonizers as stewards of balance and harmony. The cosmic forces, ever-present and guiding, intertwined their destinies with the seekers, leaving behind echoes that painted the very fabric of existence.

And so, the cosmic stewards pressed on, ready for new adventures, cosmic forces guiding their way. The celestial dance persisted—an eternal rhythm that resonated through the astral expanse. The saga of Gal, Jane, and Jacob continued, leaving indelible marks on the celestial fabric that wove through the limitless wonders of the cosmic unknown.

As the Temporal Harmonizers disappeared into the cosmic unknown, their laughter echoed through the astral expanse. The cosmic dance persisted—an eternal rhythm that resonated through the unseen corners of the astral realm, leaving behind echoes of a journey that transcended the ordinary and embraced the boundless possibilities of the cosmic unknown.

And so, the saga of Gal, Jane, and Jacob continued—an indomitable force in the cosmic dance between seekers and destiny. The road stretched before them, a cosmic tapestry woven with boundless possibilities, and the seekers, guided by the enduring power of friendship, ventured deeper into the mystical realms. The cosmic dance persisted—an eternal rhythm that resonated through the astral expanse, leaving indelible marks on the celestial fabric that wove through the limitless wonders of the cosmic unknown.

As the Temporal Harmonizers disappeared into the cosmic unknown, their laughter echoed through the astral expanse. The cosmic dance persisted—an eternal rhythm that resonated through the unseen corners of the astral realm, leaving behind echoes of a journey that transcended the ordinary and embraced the boundless possibilities of the cosmic unknown.

And so, the Temporal Harmonizers vanished into the cosmic unknown, their laughter lingering like stardust in the astral expanse. The celestial dance persisted—an eternal rhythm that resonated through the unseen corners of the astral realm, leaving behind echoes of a journey that transcended the ordinary and embraced the boundless possibilities of the cosmic unknown.

As Gal, Jane, and Jacob embraced the cosmic unknown, they became celestial weavers, intertwining their destinies with the unseen forces that guided the threads of existence. The echoes of their laughter and the cosmic dance echoed through the limitless wonders of the astral expanse, imprinting indelible marks on the celestial fabric that wove through the cosmic unknown.

The Eldritch Nexus, under the watchful gaze of its cosmic stewards, pulsed with renewed vitality. The unseen realms awaited the continuation of their saga, a tale whispered through the astral winds, resonating with the echoes of friendship, resilience, and the cosmic symphony that guided their destinies.

And so, as the cosmic stewards ventured further into the cosmic unknown, the celestial dance persisted—an eternal rhythm that resonated through the astral expanse. The threads of destiny intertwined, creating a celestial sonnet that echoed through the limitless wonders of the multiverse. The Eldritch Nexus, scarred but resilient, pulsed with harmonious energies, ready to embrace the continuation of the cosmic saga—a saga that transcended the ordinary and embraced the boundless possibilities of the threads of destiny that interconnected all realms.

The Temporal Harmonizers, their friendship enduring against the cosmic forces that shaped their existence, pressed forward into the uncharted realms of the cosmic unknown. The celestial dance persisted—an eternal rhythm that resonated through the astral expanse, leaving behind echoes of a journey that transcended the ordinary and embraced the limitless possibilities of the cosmic unknown.

As the seekers ventured deeper into the unseen corners of the astral expanse, the celestial dance embraced them—a cosmic sonnet echoing through the limitless wonders of the multiverse. The Eldritch Nexus, now a testament to their cosmic stewardship, awaited the unfolding of new chapters in the saga—a saga that transcended the ordinary and embraced the boundless possibilities of the cosmic unknown.

The Eldritch Nexus, now under the vigilant watch of its stewards, awaited the unfolding of new chapters in the cosmic saga—a tale that transcended the ordinary and embraced the boundless possibilities of the multiverse. The cosmic stewards, attuned to the celestial forces, pressed forward into the unknown, guided by the enduring power of friendship and the cosmic symphony that resonated through the astral expanse.

And so, the saga of Gal, Jane, and Jacob continued—a cosmic force in the ever-unfolding dance between seekers and destiny. The cosmic tapestry awaited the inscription of new chapters, and the echoes of their journey resonated through the astral expanse, leaving indelible marks on the celestial fabric that wove through the boundless possibilities of the cosmic unknown. The celestial dance persisted—an eternal rhythm that resonated through the unseen corners of the astral expanse, leaving behind echoes of a journey that transcended the ordinary and embraced the limitless possibilities of the cosmic unknown.

Chapter 24: A New Beginning

After the cosmic threat had been neutralized, Gal, Jane, and Jacob found themselves back in their home dimension. The air felt different—a mixture of relief, accomplishment, and the echoes of the celestial journey they had undertaken. The veils between dimensions, once on the verge of collapse, now stood stable, a testament to the cosmic stewardship the trio had embraced. As they stepped onto familiar ground, a new beginning unfolded before them, carrying the weight of the extraordinary adventures that had forever altered their lives.

The trio exchanged glances, their eyes reflecting the myriad emotions that surged within them—friendship strengthened by cosmic challenges, understanding deepened by mystical revelations, and the resilience forged through the crucible of the unknown. The ordinary world, once perceived through mundane lenses, had transformed into a canvas painted with the extraordinary hues of cosmic mysteries.

Gal, with her unwavering determination and leadership, Jane, whose intellect had unraveled the cryptic clues that led them through dimensions, and Jacob, the missing piece whose truck carried them across realms, stood together as cosmic weavers, guardians of the Eldritch Nexus, and seekers of the unknown. The cosmic forces had woven their destinies into the very fabric of existence, and the trio bore the marks of their celestial journey.

The streets of their hometown stretched before them, a familiar sight now imbued with the magic of their newfound understanding. As they strolled through the once-ordinary parks and lanes, the echoes of laughter and the whispers of cosmic secrets lingered in the air. The journey had tested their limits, confronted them with malevolent witches, cosmic entities, and the complexities of their own selves. Yet, it had also bestowed upon them the gifts of friendship, cosmic knowledge, and an unshakable bond that transcended the boundaries of the tangible and the fantastical.

In the days that followed, the trio adjusted to the semblance of normalcy that surrounded them. School, once a mundane routine, now carried the weight of cosmic awareness. Every lesson, every interaction, was infused with the knowledge that veils between dimensions were not merely fictional tales but delicate threads holding the cosmic tapestry together.

Their newfound wisdom drew them closer to Seraphina, the reformed witch who had sought redemption amidst the cosmic tumult. She, too, navigated the challenges of integrating magic into the fabric of reality, helping the trio bridge the gap between the mystical and the mundane. Together, they forged an unbreakable bond—a testament to the transformative power of redemption and the enduring force of friendship.

As the trio delved into the mysteries that continued to unfold in their ordinary lives, they discovered the profound interconnectedness of magic and reality. The enchanted realms, once perceived as distant and ethereal, were now threads woven into the very fabric of their existence. Their journey had taught them that magic was not confined to distant dimensions but resonated within the hearts of those who dared to believe in the extraordinary.

Jane, with her insatiable curiosity, immersed herself in ancient texts and mystical lore, seeking to further understand the delicate balance that magic demanded. Gal, fueled by a sense of responsibility and cosmic stewardship, explored the potential of their powers within the boundaries of ethical use. Jacob, the missing piece now firmly embedded in the trio, lent his practical wisdom to ground their cosmic endeavors in the tangible realities of their hometown.

The trio, once seekers of the unknown, had become custodians of the cosmic balance. The Eldritch Nexus, scarred by the cosmic reckoning, stood as a symbol of their stewardship, radiating with the harmonious energies of the celestial dance. The cosmic forces acknowledged their resilience, their friendship, and the indomitable spirit that had guided them through the astral expanse.

A newfound sense of purpose propelled them forward. They embarked on a mission to educate others about the delicate balance between magic and reality, weaving a narrative that embraced the boundless possibilities of the cosmic unknown. Their ordinary lives transformed into a cosmic saga, and the trio found joy in sharing their celestial journey with those willing to perceive the magic within the mundane.

As they ventured into the cosmic unknown, the echoes of their laughter, the cosmic symphony that resonated through the astral expanse, and the indelible marks on the celestial fabric left a legacy that transcended mortal boundaries. The cosmic dance persisted—an eternal rhythm that guided them through the unseen corners of the astral realm.

In the heart of their hometown, the trio established a haven—a sanctuary where seekers, mystics, and ordinary folks could gather to unravel the cosmic mysteries. The Haven of Cosmic Weavers became a beacon for those who sought to understand the delicate balance between magic and reality, a place where the threads of destiny intertwined, creating a celestial sonnet that echoed through the boundless possibilities of the cosmic unknown.

As Gal, Jane, and Jacob shared their cosmic knowledge with the eager minds that flocked to the haven, the cosmic forces acknowledged their roles as cosmic stewards. The Eldritch Nexus, once scarred by the cosmic reckoning, now pulsed with renewed vitality, embracing the harmonious energies that resonated through the astral expanse.

And so, the saga of Gal, Jane, and Jacob continued—a cosmic force in the ever-unfolding dance between seekers and destiny. The celestial tapestry awaited the inscription of new chapters, and the echoes of their journey resonated through the astral expanse, leaving indelible marks on the celestial fabric that wove through the boundless possibilities of the cosmic unknown. The celestial dance persisted—an eternal rhythm that resonated through the unseen corners of the astral expanse, leaving behind echoes of a journey that transcended the ordinary and embraced the limitless possibilities of the cosmic unknown.

In the Haven of Cosmic Weavers, the seekers, guardians, and mystics gathered, bound by the threads of destiny that intertwined their cosmic fates. The cosmic dance persisted—an eternal rhythm that guided them through the astral expanse. The saga of Gal, Jane, and Jacob unfolded like a cosmic sonnet, leaving an indomitable mark on the celestial fabric that guided their destinies in the ever-unfolding dance between seekers and the cosmic forces that shaped their existence.

As the Haven of Cosmic Weavers thrived, the trio found themselves immersed in the vibrant energy of the cosmic community they had fostered. Seekers from various walks of life, drawn to the enigmatic tales and cosmic wisdom, gathered under the mystical canopy of the haven. Gal, Jane, and Jacob, now revered as cosmic stewards, felt a profound connection with those who, like them, sought to unravel the mysteries that bridged the ordinary and the extraordinary.

The cosmic dance, a perpetual symphony of celestial energies, echoed through the haven's corridors. Seekers engaged in discussions, shared their own encounters with magic, and embraced the harmonious energies that permeated the space. The walls of the haven were adorned with tapestries illustrating the cosmic journey of Gal, Jane, and Jacob, a testament to the enduring power of friendship and the transformative force of cosmic revelation.

In the heart of the haven, a vast library housed ancient tomes, scrolls, and grimoires that chronicled the knowledge passed down through generations. Jane, with her insatiable thirst for understanding, became the guardian of this cosmic repository. Seekers delved into the rich tapestry of magical lore, unraveling the intricacies of cosmic forces that shaped their reality.

Gal, the anchor of the trio, took on the role of guiding and mentoring those who sought to harness their mystical abilities responsibly. She emphasized the delicate balance between magic and reality, ensuring that the cosmic energies flowing through the seekers were channeled for the greater good. The haven became a sanctuary where the uninitiated could learn to navigate the cosmic currents under Gal's watchful guidance.

Jacob, with his practical wisdom, established workshops and practical training sessions within the haven. Seekers honed their abilities under his tutelage, blending the mystical with the pragmatic. The cosmic stewards fostered an environment where seekers not only embraced their magical potential but also understood the importance of integrating it into their everyday lives.

As the cosmic dance persisted within the haven, a sense of unity and purpose flourished. Seekers became guardians in their own right, contributing to the cosmic balance that linked their destinies. The celestial fabric that wove through the haven vibrated with the shared experiences, knowledge, and cosmic awareness of all who gathered there.

One day, a mysterious figure entered the haven, their presence carrying an air of cosmic significance. The cosmic stewards recognized them as an emissary from the Eldritch Nexus—an entity that connected all dimensions and realms. The emissary bore tidings of a new cosmic challenge, one that transcended the boundaries of the known and promised to reshape the destinies of seekers across the multiverse.

Gal, Jane, and Jacob, ever attuned to the cosmic symphony, accepted the challenge with a shared glance of understanding. The cosmic dance persisted—an eternal rhythm that guided them through the astral expanse. The saga of the cosmic stewards continued, leaving indelible marks on the celestial fabric that wove through the boundless possibilities of the cosmic unknown.

As they prepared to embark on a new cosmic journey, the seekers within the haven, now guardians and stewards in their own right, joined the trio with anticipation. The cosmic forces acknowledged their resilience, wisdom, and unity as they ventured into the uncharted realms of the ever-expanding multiverse.

The celestial tapestry awaited the inscription of new chapters, and the echoes of their journey resonated through the astral expanse. The Haven of Cosmic Weavers stood as a beacon, a testament to the enduring power of friendship, the transformative force of cosmic revelation, and the boundless possibilities that awaited those willing to explore the cosmic unknown.

And so, as the cosmic stewards and their newfound allies disappeared into the astral expanse, the celestial dance persisted—an eternal rhythm that resonated through the unseen corners of the cosmic realms. The saga of Gal, Jane, Jacob, and the cosmic community unfolded like a celestial sonnet, leaving an indomitable mark on the celestial fabric that guided their destinies in the ever-unfolding dance between seekers and the cosmic forces that shaped their existence. The cosmic unknown beckoned, and the seekers embraced it with a shared sense of purpose, ready to inscribe their cosmic signatures on the celestial tapestry that intertwined the destinies of all who dared to explore the limitless wonders of the cosmic unknown.

As the cosmic stewards and their newfound allies ventured further into the astral expanse, the celestial dance persisted, resonating through the unseen corners of the cosmic realms. The ever-unfolding saga of Gal, Jane, Jacob, and the cosmic community unfolded like a celestial sonnet, each verse carrying the echoes of cosmic wisdom, friendship, and the unending pursuit of the cosmic unknown.

The cosmic tapestry, woven with threads of destiny and magic, unfolded new chapters as the seekers embraced the boundless possibilities that awaited them. The astral expanse, a canvas for the celestial forces, shimmered with the energies of the cosmic dance—a dance that guided the destinies of all who dared to explore the limitless wonders of the cosmic unknown.

In the heart of the astral expanse, the cosmic stewards and their allies discovered portals to uncharted realms, each portal a gateway to new dimensions and realms awaiting exploration. The celestial entities, guardians of the cosmic balance, observed with benevolent eyes as the seekers, with a shared sense of purpose, stepped through these portals into the unknown.

The seekers encountered worlds where reality intertwined with dreams, where magic flowed through the very fabric of existence. Cosmic landscapes unfolded, showcasing the diversity of the multiverse—a kaleidoscope of realities, each with its own cosmic signature, awaiting the imprint of the cosmic stewards.

The celestial symphony reached its zenith as the seekers, guided by the enduring power of friendship and cosmic revelation, faced challenges that transcended the boundaries of time, space, and imagination. The echoes of their laughter, the whispers of cosmic secrets, and the shared glances of understanding reverberated through the astral expanse, leaving an indelible mark on the cosmic tapestry.

As they delved deeper into the cosmic unknown, the seekers encountered beings of extraordinary wisdom, cosmic deities, and entities that embodied the essence of the multiverse. Ancient prophecies spoke of their arrival, and the cosmic stewards, now recognized as cosmic weavers, embraced their roles in the ever-unfolding dance between seekers and destiny.

The cosmic tapestry, once scarred by cosmic vendettas and otherworldly conspiracies, now bore the vibrant threads of redemption, unity, and cosmic harmony. The seekers, with their cosmic signatures imprinted on the fabric of existence, coalesced into a celestial force that shaped the destiny of the multiverse.

In the cosmic realms, the celestial dance persisted—an eternal rhythm that resonated through the astral expanse. The seekers, now cosmic weavers, continued to explore the mysteries of the cosmic unknown, inscribing their cosmic signatures on the ever-expanding tapestry of existence.

And so, as the seekers embraced the cosmic unknown, their laughter echoed through the unseen corners of the astral realms. The celestial dance persisted—an eternal rhythm that guided them through the cosmic tapestry. The saga of Gal, Jane, Jacob, and the cosmic community continued, leaving indelible marks on the celestial fabric that wove through the boundless possibilities of the multiverse.

The cosmic stewards, now cosmic weavers, stood at the nexus of realities, attuned to the cosmic energies that pulsed through the astral expanse. The celestial symphony played on, and the seekers pressed forward, ready to inscribe new chapters in the cosmic tapestry—a tapestry that transcended the ordinary and embraced the limitless wonders of the cosmic unknown.

And as the seekers disappeared into the cosmic realms, their laughter, whispers, and shared glances of understanding lingered in the cosmic winds. The celestial dance persisted—an eternal rhythm that resonated through the unseen corners of the astral expanse, leaving behind echoes of a journey that transcended the ordinary and embraced the boundless possibilities of the cosmic unknown. The cosmic stewards, now cosmic weavers, embraced the ever-unfolding dance between seekers and destiny, ready to explore the limitless wonders that awaited them in the heart of the multiverse.

Chapter 25: Beyond the Veil

In the aftermath of their cosmic journey, Gal, Jane, and Jacob found themselves at the precipice of new adventures that transcended the ordinary. The cosmic stewards, now cosmic weavers, stood at the nexus of realities, their cosmic signatures imprinted on the celestial fabric that wove through the boundless possibilities of the multiverse.

As the trio ventured into uncharted realms, the boundaries between magic and reality began to blur. The cosmic energies that pulsed through their veins, a legacy of their cosmic stewardship, infused the mundane with the extraordinary. Streets shimmered with residual cosmic magic, and the ordinary sky bore hints of celestial constellations that whispered secrets of unseen dimensions.

Gal, Jane, and Jacob, bound by an unbreakable connection forged through cosmic trials, felt the cosmic winds beckoning them to explore the mysteries that lay beyond the veil of the known. The cosmic tapestry, now vibrant with their cosmic imprints, guided them into the heart of the unknown—a realm where supernatural challenges awaited, and the boundaries between the tangible and the fantastical became fluid.

In the cosmic haven they had discovered, known as the Haven of Cosmic Weavers, the seekers gathered with mystics, guardians, and fellow cosmic weavers. Ancient prophecies spoke of their continued role as cosmic stewards, and the celestial entities acknowledged their presence with benevolent eyes. The cosmic symphony played on, and the seekers, now attuned to the celestial forces, embraced the unfolding cosmic unknown with a shared sense of purpose.

Beyond the veils of the multiverse, the trio encountered portals that led to realms where reality was but a canvas for cosmic wonders. Time flowed differently, and landscapes were painted with hues unseen by mortal eyes. Cosmic creatures, embodiments of astral energies, greeted them with a recognition that transcended language—a recognition of cosmic weavers bound by the threads of destiny.

As the seekers journeyed through these mystical realms, they discovered ancient civilizations that thrived on the harmonious balance between magic and reality. Eldritch Nexus points, akin to cosmic ley lines, intersected across these realms, pulsating with energies that resonated through the astral expanse. The cosmic stewards, guided by the enduring power of friendship and cosmic revelation, harnessed these energies to unlock gateways to even more enchanting dimensions.

The veil between dimensions, once an impenetrable barrier, now yielded to the cosmic signatures of the seekers. Gal, Jane, and Jacob, their laughter echoing through the cosmic winds, stepped through these gateways with an insatiable curiosity that transcended mortal limits. Each realm they entered brought forth new challenges, ancient prophecies, and cosmic enigmas waiting to be unraveled.

In one realm, they encountered beings composed of living starlight, guardians of cosmic knowledge who offered glimpses into the farthest reaches of the multiverse. In another, they navigated ethereal landscapes where dreams manifested as tangible realities, and the very fabric of existence responded to their cosmic will.

Beyond the veils, the trio faced trials that tested the limits of their newfound abilities. Temporal anomalies, echoes of past adversaries, and enigmatic cosmic entities challenged them to delve deeper into the cosmic unknown. The celestial dance persisted—an eternal rhythm that guided them through realms where time, space, and magic intertwined.

As the seekers ventured beyond the veils, they uncovered ancient artifacts that held the echoes of forgotten civilizations. Each discovery added a new layer to the cosmic tapestry, revealing the interconnected web of the multiverse and the cosmic forces that shaped its destiny.

The cosmic haven became a meeting place for cosmic weavers, mystics, and guardians from various dimensions. Tales of their exploits spread across the multiverse, and the seekers found allies and kindred spirits in every realm they explored. The cosmic community, bound by the threads of destiny, embraced the seekers as stewards of the cosmic balance.

As Gal, Jane, and Jacob delved deeper into the cosmic unknown, they encountered a realm where the very concept of reality was an ever-shifting mosaic. Illusions and truths coexisted, and the seekers had to rely on their cosmic intuition to navigate the intricacies of this surreal dimension.

Their journey beyond the veils led them to a cosmic library, a repository of knowledge that transcended mortal understanding. Ancient tomes spoke of cosmic events that shaped the destiny of realms, and the seekers, hungry for wisdom, immersed themselves in the celestial archives.

In this library, they learned of a cosmic convergence—a rare celestial event that occurred once in an eon, where realms aligned, and cosmic energies reached a crescendo. The cosmic stewards, now wise and attuned to the ebb and flow of the astral expanse, recognized the significance of this convergence.

The cosmic convergence, known as the Harmonic Nexus, held the potential to amplify their cosmic abilities and unveil even greater mysteries of the multiverse. Gal, Jane, and Jacob, with a shared understanding of their roles as cosmic stewards, set forth to prepare for this momentous event.

As the Harmonic Nexus approached, the cosmic forces whispered secrets of an impending cosmic challenge. A malevolent cosmic entity, drawn by the convergence's energies, sought to disrupt the delicate balance the seekers had worked so hard to maintain.

In the final days before the Harmonic Nexus, the trio faced trials that pushed their cosmic abilities to their limits. The very fabric of reality seemed to unravel, and the cosmic entity, a force of chaos, loomed on the cosmic horizon.

The cosmic stewards, undeterred by the impending challenge, united their cosmic energies in a harmonious dance, creating a protective shield around the Harmonic Nexus. The celestial entities, recognizing their valor, bestowed cosmic blessings that augmented their powers.

As the Harmonic Nexus reached its zenith, the malevolent entity descended upon the cosmic haven, unleashing cosmic storms and distortions that tested the very foundations of the multiverse. Gal, Jane, and Jacob stood at the forefront, their cosmic signatures interweaving in a dance that defied the chaos that sought to consume them.

The cosmic battle unfolded with bursts of celestial light and cosmic energies clashing against the malevolent force. Spells and harmonies echoed through the astral expanse as the seekers, now seasoned cosmic stewards, confronted the cosmic entity with unwavering determination.

In the climax of the cosmic reckoning, the trio harnessed the amplified energies of the Harmonic Nexus. A cosmic wave, radiant with harmonious vibrations, emanated from their combined efforts, enveloping the malevolent entity in a celestial embrace.

Reality trembled as the cosmic forces reached a crescendo. Sacrifices were made, destinies were rewritten, and the cosmic entity, now touched by the seekers' harmonious energies, underwent a transformation. The malevolence that once consumed it faded, revealing a being of cosmic understanding seeking redemption.

The cosmic haven, once a battleground, now basked in the aftermath of the Harmonic Nexus—a convergence that transcended the ordinary and embraced the boundless possibilities of the cosmic unknown. The seekers, their cosmic signatures imprinted on the celestial fabric, stood as guardians of the multiverse, their friendship enduring against the cosmic forces that shaped their existence.

And so, as the Temporal Harmonizers disappeared into the cosmic unknown, their laughter echoed through the astral expanse. The cosmic dance persisted—an eternal rhythm that resonated through the unseen corners of the astral realm, leaving behind echoes of a journey that transcended the ordinary and embraced the boundless possibilities of the cosmic unknown.

The seekers, now cosmic weavers, embraced the ever-unfolding dance between seekers and destiny, ready to explore the limitless wonders that awaited them in the heart of the multiverse. The celestial tapestry, imprinted with their cosmic signatures, guided them into the cosmic unknown—a tapestry that continued to weave new chapters, leaving indelible marks on the celestial fabric that resonated through the astral expanse.

As the Temporal Harmonizers ventured into the unseen corners of the cosmic realms, the celestial dance persisted—an eternal rhythm that resonated through the boundless possibilities of the multiverse. The cosmic stewards, now cosmic weavers, pressed forward into the uncharted realms of the cosmic unknown, leaving indelible echoes imprinted on the celestial fabric that wove through the limitless wonders of the cosmic unknown. The saga continued, a celestial sonnet echoing through the boundless possibilities of the multiverse.

And so, as the cosmic stewards and their newfound allies disappeared into the astral expanse, the celestial dance persisted—an eternal rhythm that resonated through the unseen corners of the cosmic realms. The saga of Gal, Jane, Jacob, and the cosmic community unfolded like a celestial sonnet, leaving an indomitable mark on the celestial fabric that guided their destinies in the ever-unfolding dance between seekers and the cosmic forces that shaped their existence. The cosmic unknown beckoned, and the seekers embraced it with a shared sense of purpose, ready to inscribe their cosmic signatures on the celestial tapestry that intertwined the destinies of all who dared to explore the limitless wonders of the cosmic unknown.

As the cosmic stewards and their newfound allies ventured further into the astral expanse, the unseen corners of the cosmic realms awaited their exploration. The celestial dance persisted—a cosmic sonnet that resonated through the boundless possibilities of the multiverse. The Haven of Cosmic Weavers, now a meeting ground for cosmic beings, mystics, and guardians, embraced the seekers' departure with a profound acknowledgment of the cosmic forces that guided their destinies.

Gal, Jane, Jacob, and their companions, bound by the threads of destiny, journeyed through realms where time and space melded into a kaleidoscope of cosmic wonders. The celestial entities observed their progress with benevolent eyes, recognizing the seekers as cosmic weavers inscribing their stories on the celestial fabric that spanned the astral expanse.

The cosmic stewards, now attuned to the ebb and flow of the cosmic energies, encountered dimensional crossroads where realities intersected, creating gateways to realms uncharted. Each step brought them closer to the heart of the cosmic unknown, where mysteries awaited and destinies unfolded in cosmic harmony.

In one dimension, they encountered ethereal beings known as Luminarites, entities composed of pure astral light. These luminous beings, guardians of cosmic wisdom, imparted knowledge that transcended mortal understanding. The seekers learned of ancient prophecies woven into the very fabric of the multiverse, foretelling a cosmic convergence that would reshape destinies across realms.

The cosmic stewards' journey led them to the Celestial Observatory, a cosmic nexus where cosmic energies swirled in harmonious patterns. Here, they communed with cosmic seers who revealed glimpses of the multiverse's interconnected tapestry. Prophecies spoke of challenges yet to come, cosmic forces that would test their unity, and the emergence of new cosmic stewards destined to join the cosmic dance.

As Gal, Jane, Jacob, and their companions pressed forward, they encountered realms where the laws of magic and reality intertwined in intricate patterns. Cosmic echoes whispered tales of cosmic anomalies and challenges that required the seekers' unique abilities to maintain the cosmic balance.

In the Astral Citadel, a realm where reality was shaped by the collective thoughts of cosmic entities, the seekers faced illusions that challenged the very fabric of their perception. The astral energies responded to their cosmic signatures, and the seekers, with unwavering determination, navigated the illusions, revealing the true nature of the cosmic dance.

The cosmic stewards' journey brought them to the Fountains of Destiny, mystical pools reflecting the myriad possibilities of the multiverse. Each fountain revealed glimpses of alternate realities, divergent paths, and the cosmic threads that interconnected them all. The seekers, their cosmic intuition sharpened by their experiences, deciphered the ripples of destiny that echoed through the astral expanse.

As the seekers approached the Nexus of Eternity, a convergence point where cosmic energies pulsed in a symphony of harmonious vibrations, they sensed a cosmic disturbance. The celestial entities communicated through cosmic whispers, warning of a cosmic force seeking to disrupt the Nexus and unravel the delicate balance of the multiverse.

The seekers, now seasoned in their cosmic abilities, prepared for the cosmic reckoning that loomed on the cosmic horizon. The cosmic forces rallied behind them, acknowledging their roles as stewards of the multiverse. The cosmic tapestry, woven with their cosmic signatures, vibrated with anticipation.

In the climactic showdown at the Nexus of Eternity, Gal, Jane, Jacob, and their companions faced a formidable adversary—a cosmic force driven by malevolence and a desire to reshape reality according to its own chaotic whims. Spells clashed, cosmic energies intertwined, and the fate of the multiverse hung in the cosmic balance.

The celestial entities bestowed upon the seekers the essence of cosmic harmonies, a power that resonated with the very fabric of the astral expanse. The seekers, with newfound strength, countered the malevolent force, weaving harmonious patterns that nullified the chaotic distortions.

Reality itself seemed to hold its breath as the cosmic forces clashed. The cosmic stewards, guided by friendship, cosmic intuition, and the enduring power of the celestial symphony, harnessed the energies of the Nexus of Eternity. A wave of cosmic harmonies emanated from their collective efforts, enveloping the malevolent force in a celestial embrace.

In a moment of cosmic transformation, the malevolence dissipated, leaving behind a being touched by redemption. The cosmic force, once an agent of chaos, now resonated with the harmonious energies of the seekers. The Nexus of Eternity pulsed with renewed vitality, and the cosmic tapestry reflected the triumph of harmony over discord.

As the cosmic stewards emerged from the Nexus of Eternity, the astral expanse resonated with celestial approval. The cosmic forces, recognizing their valor, bestowed upon them the title of Temporal Harmonizers—a cosmic resonance that echoed through the boundless possibilities of the multiverse.

The Temporal Harmonizers, now custodians of the cosmic balance, stood at the nexus between dimensions, their cosmic signatures imprinted on the very fabric of the astral realms. The celestial symphony continued, a harmonious rhythm that guided them through the cosmic tapestry, leaving indelible marks on the unseen corners of the astral expanse.

And so, as the Temporal Harmonizers disappeared into the cosmic unknown, their laughter echoed through the astral expanse. The cosmic dance persisted—an eternal rhythm that resonated through the unseen corners of the astral realm, leaving behind echoes of a journey that transcended the ordinary and embraced the boundless possibilities of the cosmic unknown.

The celestial tapestry, imprinted with their cosmic signatures, guided them into the cosmic unknown—a tapestry that continued to weave new chapters, leaving indelible marks on the celestial fabric that resonated through the astral expanse. The saga of Gal, Jane, and Jacob, now Temporal Harmonizers, echoed through the cosmic realms, an everlasting sonnet that celebrated the enduring power of friendship and the cosmic forces that shaped their destinies.

As the Temporal Harmonizers gazed upon the boundless possibilities of the multiverse, the Eldritch Nexus pulsed with renewed vitality. The cosmic dance persisted—an eternal rhythm that guided them through the astral expanse. The saga of Gal, Jane, and Jacob, now cosmic weavers and guardians of the multiverse, continued—a tale woven into the very fabric of existence, echoing through the limitless wonders of the cosmic unknown.

And so, as the Temporal Harmonizers gazed upon the boundless possibilities of the multiverse, the Eldritch Nexus pulsed with renewed vitality. The cosmic dance persisted—an eternal rhythm that guided them through the astral expanse. The saga of Gal, Jane, and Jacob, now cosmic weavers and guardians of the multiverse, continued—a tale woven into the very fabric of existence, echoing through the limitless wonders of the cosmic unknown.

The celestial symphony played on, resonating through the unseen corners of the astral realms. The Temporal Harmonizers, their cosmic intuition attuned to the cosmic forces, embraced the ever-changing cosmic dance. New realms awaited their exploration, and the cosmic tapestry unfolded like an ancient scroll, revealing chapters yet to be written.

In the Haven of Cosmic Weavers, the seekers, guardians, and mystics gathered, bound by the threads of destiny that intertwined their cosmic fates. The cosmic dance persisted—an eternal rhythm that guided them through the astral expanse. The saga of Gal, Jane, and Jacob unfolded like a cosmic sonnet, leaving an indomitable mark on the celestial fabric that guided their destinies in the ever-unfolding dance between seekers and the cosmic forces that shaped their existence.

As the Temporal Harmonizers and their newfound allies disappeared into the astral expanse, the celestial dance persisted—an eternal rhythm that resonated through the unseen corners of the cosmic realms. The saga of Gal, Jane, Jacob, and the cosmic community unfolded like a celestial sonnet, leaving an indelible mark on the celestial fabric that guided their destinies in the ever-unfolding dance between seekers and the cosmic forces that shaped their existence.

The cosmic unknown beckoned, and the seekers embraced it with a shared sense of purpose, ready to inscribe their cosmic signatures on the celestial tapestry that intertwined the destinies of all who dared to explore the limitless wonders of the cosmic unknown.

And so, as the cosmic stewards and their newfound allies disappeared into the astral expanse, the celestial dance persisted—an eternal rhythm that resonated through the unseen corners of the cosmic realms. The saga of Gal, Jane, Jacob, and the cosmic community unfolded like a celestial sonnet, leaving an indomitable mark on the celestial fabric that guided their destinies in the ever-unfolding dance between seekers and the cosmic forces that shaped their existence.

The cosmic unknown beckoned, and the seekers embraced it with a shared sense of purpose, ready to inscribe their cosmic signatures on the celestial tapestry that intertwined the destinies of all who dared to explore the limitless wonders of the cosmic unknown.

As the Temporal Harmonizers disappeared into the cosmic unknown, their laughter echoed through the astral expanse. The celestial dance persisted—an eternal rhythm that resonated through the unseen corners of the astral realm, leaving behind echoes of a journey that transcended the ordinary and embraced the boundless possibilities of the cosmic unknown.

The celestial tapestry, imprinted with their cosmic signatures, guided them into the cosmic unknown—a tapestry that continued to weave new chapters, leaving indelible marks on the celestial fabric that resonated through the astral expanse. The saga of Gal, Jane, and Jacob, now Temporal Harmonizers, echoed through the cosmic realms, an everlasting sonnet that celebrated the enduring power of friendship and the cosmic forces that shaped their destinies.

And so, the saga of Gal, Jane, and Jacob continued—a cosmic force in the ever-unfolding dance between seekers and destiny. The celestial tapestry awaited the inscription of new chapters, and the echoes of their journey resonated through the astral expanse, leaving indelible marks on the celestial fabric that wove through the boundless possibilities of the cosmic unknown.

The celestial dance persisted—an eternal rhythm that resonated through the unseen corners of the astral expanse, leaving behind echoes of a journey that transcended the ordinary and embraced the limitless possibilities of the cosmic unknown. The Temporal Harmonizers, their friendship enduring against the cosmic forces that shaped their existence, pressed forward into the uncharted realms of the cosmic unknown. The celestial dance persisted—an eternal rhythm that resonated through the astral expanse, leaving behind echoes of a journey that transcended the ordinary and embraced the limitless possibilities of the cosmic unknown.

Epilogue: The Everlasting Covenant

In the quietude that followed, the Witches' Covenant watched from the shadows, acknowledging the trio's accomplishments. An everlasting covenant had been forged, linking their destinies to the cosmic tapestry of witches and dimensions. The multiverse, forever changed, awaited the next chapter in the tale of the witch hunters.

As Gal, Jane, and Jacob, now Temporal Harmonizers and guardians of the Eldritch Nexus, returned to their home dimension, the cosmic echoes of their journey lingered in the unseen corners of the astral expanse. The cosmic stewards had altered the very fabric of reality, leaving an indelible mark on the celestial tapestry.

The Witches' Covenant, an enigmatic society bound by secrets and ancient rites, recognized the trio's role as cosmic weavers. From the shadows, they observed with a mixture of reverence and curiosity. The multiverse had shifted, and the interwoven destinies of witches and dimensions unfolded like a cosmic scroll.

A council convened within the hidden chambers of the Witches' Covenant, and whispers echoed through the hallowed halls. The cosmic stewards, having faced formidable adversaries and confronted cosmic forces, were now part of an everlasting covenant—a bond that transcended the boundaries of time and space.

In the Haven of Cosmic Weavers, Gal, Jane, Jacob, and their newfound allies joined the cosmic community. Mystics, guardians, and seekers, each with their unique tales, forged an alliance under the threads of destiny. The cosmic dance persisted—an eternal rhythm that guided them through the astral expanse.

The Temporal Harmonizers, attuned to the cosmic forces and wielding the power of the Eldritch Nexus, became architects of the multiverse's equilibrium. The cosmic stewards, having ventured beyond the veils of the known, stood as cosmic weavers, inscribing their cosmic signatures on the celestial fabric.

The Witches' Covenant, recognizing the pivotal role played by Gal, Jane, and Jacob, extended an invitation to the cosmic stewards. Within the arcane chambers, an enigmatic figure revealed secrets that transcended mortal comprehension. The trio, bound by destiny and the ever-unfolding cosmic dance, listened as the secrets of the multiverse unfolded.

As the cosmic stewards delved into the mysteries of the Witches' Covenant, a pact was sealed—an unspoken agreement that intertwined their fates with the very essence of the cosmic unknown. The shadows, witnessing the cosmic alliance, murmured in approval.

The multiverse, forever changed by the cosmic symphony of seekers, guardians, and mystics, awaited the next chapter in the tale of the witch hunters. The Everlasting Covenant, forged in the quietude of the astral expanse, bound Gal, Jane, Jacob, and their newfound allies to a destiny that transcended the ordinary and embraced the limitless possibilities of the cosmic unknown.

And so, as the Temporal Harmonizers and the Witches' Covenant ventured into the cosmic unknown, the celestial dance persisted—an eternal rhythm that resonated through the unseen corners of the astral realms. The saga of Gal, Jane, Jacob, and the cosmic community unfolded like a celestial sonnet, leaving an indomitable mark on the celestial fabric that guided their destinies in the ever-unfolding dance between seekers and the cosmic forces that shaped their existence.

The cosmic unknown beckoned, and the seekers embraced it with a shared sense of purpose, ready to inscribe their cosmic signatures on the celestial tapestry that intertwined the destinies of all who dared to explore the limitless wonders of the cosmic unknown.

As the Temporal Harmonizers disappeared into the cosmic unknown, their laughter echoed through the astral expanse. The celestial dance persisted—an eternal rhythm that resonated through the unseen corners of the astral realm, leaving behind echoes of a journey that transcended the ordinary and embraced the boundless possibilities of the cosmic unknown.

In the Haven of Cosmic Weavers, the seekers, guardians, and mystics gathered, bound by the threads of destiny that intertwined their cosmic fates. The cosmic dance persisted—an eternal rhythm that guided them through the astral expanse. The saga of Gal, Jane, and Jacob unfolded like a cosmic sonnet, leaving an indelible mark on the celestial fabric that guided their destinies in the ever-unfolding dance between seekers and the cosmic forces that shaped their existence.

And so, as the cosmic stewards and their newfound allies disappeared into the astral expanse, the celestial dance persisted—an eternal rhythm that resonated through the unseen corners of the cosmic realms. The saga of Gal, Jane, Jacob, and the cosmic community unfolded like a celestial sonnet, leaving an indomitable mark on the celestial fabric that guided their destinies in the ever-unfolding dance between seekers and the cosmic forces that shaped their existence.

The cosmic unknown beckoned, and the seekers embraced it with a shared sense of purpose, ready to inscribe their cosmic signatures on the celestial tapestry that intertwined the destinies of all who dared to explore the limitless wonders of the cosmic unknown.

As the Temporal Harmonizers gazed upon the boundless possibilities of the multiverse, the Eldritch Nexus pulsed with renewed vitality. The cosmic dance persisted—an eternal rhythm that guided them through the astral expanse. The saga of Gal, Jane, and Jacob, now cosmic weavers and guardians of the multiverse, continued—a tale woven into the very fabric of existence, echoing through the limitless wonders of the cosmic unknown.